Spiced Latte

Killer

Book Ten in
The INNcredibly Sweet Series
By

Summer Prescott

Author's note: I'd love to hear your thoughts on my books, the storylines, and anything else that you'd like to comment on—reader feedback is very important to me. My contact information, along with some other helpful links, is listed below. If you'd like to be on my list of "folks to contact" with updates, release and sales notifications, etc.… just shoot me an email and let me know. Thanks for reading!

Also…

… if you're looking for more great reads, I am proud to announce that Summer Prescott Books publishes a popular series by new cozy author Patti Benning. Check out my book catalog http://summerprescottbooks.com/book-catalog/ for her delicious stories.

Contact Info for Summer Prescott:

Twitter: @summerprescott1

Blog and Book Catalog:
http://summerprescottbooks.com

Email: summer.prescott.cozies@gmail.com

Please note: If you receive any correspondence from addresses other than those listed here, it is not from me, even if it claims to be.

And... look me up on Facebook—let's be friends!

If you're an author and are interested in publishing with Summer Prescott Books, please send me an email and I'll send you submission guidelines.

ACKNOWLEDGEMENTS:

This book was a difficult journey for me. I began writing it just before I went to visit my mother, who is waging war against cancer. For the two weeks that I soaked in the California sunshine, while helping to care for the woman who has spent her life caring for me, I set aside everything else in my life – writing, business, everything – and I don't regret it for a moment.

Returning home, it was difficult to get back into the swing of things, but with a tremendous amount of effort and encouragement, I was finally able to immerse myself in the sweet and mysterious world of Missy and Chas. There are several times while writing this book, that I laughed and cried with the characters, and the losses that they felt at times resonated with me in a way that seemed to transcend the connection between an author and her characters.

It was powerful for me, and I hope that it will, at the very least, be entertaining for you. If it touches your heart, I'm thankful, because in the grand scheme of things, isn't that what life is all about? Giving ourselves over to the things that move us is what makes us human, and what makes us connect with the things that are so important – love, relationships, the pain of loss, and the triumph of rebuilding.

Hug the ones you love, and live life to the fullest while you have breath in your lungs and love in your heart, because we never know what tomorrow may bring.

This book is dedicated to one of the most loving, giving and courageous people I know…my beautiful mother.

SPICED LATTE

KILLER

Book Ten in The INNcredibly Sweet Series

TABLE OF CONTENTS

CHAPTER 1

Melissa Gladstone-Beckett slid the last batch of pumpkin spice latte cupcakes into the oven. The small commercial kitchen at Cupcakes in Paradise smelled amazing, reminding her of many beautiful autumns that she'd spent in her hometown of LaChance, Louisiana. She was in Florida now—with Detective Chas Beckett, her handsome and clever husband—but she still felt pangs of homesickness every now and again. The happy couple had moved to the sleepy beachside community of Calgon, Florida, after they'd gotten married just over a year ago, and had purchased a bed and breakfast inn on the beach, turning the cozy little cottage next door into a cupcake shop a few months later.

Missy had owned two cupcake shops when she lived in Louisiana, one in LaChance, and the other in a neighboring town, Dellville. For the last few months, she'd been planning the wedding of one of her former managers who was like a son to her; suddenly, his bride-to-be had come up missing. Missy had a long-standing habit of baking whenever she was stressed out, and the pumpkin cupcakes that she had just finished up were the last in a long line of baked goods that her cozy kitchen had generated that morning.

Missy was worried about Sarah, the lovely young fiancée of her former manager Grayson, but was waiting with great hope for the good news that she'd been found. The couple's wedding was a week away, and Grayson's bride had simply disappeared. It wasn't like her to go away without saying anything, particularly this close to the happiest day of her life. Grayson was a pale, dark-haired, quiet young man, who'd found his soulmate in Sarah's sweet honesty, and the two of them had been ecstatic to announce their engagement.

The chimes over the front door jangled, jarring the petite blonde cupcake shop owner out of her reverie. She hoped that it signaled the arrival of her free-spirited, fiery-haired friend, Echo Kellerman. Echo was recently married, and pregnant with her first child, which sometimes made for a very cranky bestie, but Missy indulged her moods, knowing that this too would pass.

As expected, Echo had flopped into a chair at their favorite bistro table in the eating area, as was customary on most mornings. The two of them started most days with conversation, coffee and cupcakes before venturing out into the real world. On occasion, Echo's new husband, Phillip "Kel" Kellerman, would join them, bringing them up to speed on local events and juicy gossip. Kel had been born and raised in Calgon and seemed to know everyone and everything of consequence in the town. He took it upon himself to share his knowledge with Missy and Echo, the relative newcomers, and regaled them with tales of life, relationships, deaths, and divorce, as well as mergers and other business matters taking place within the comfortable confines of Calgon.

"How ya feelin', darlin?" Missy asked, planting a kiss on the top of her best friend's head before sitting down across from her.

"Well, I can finally eat without fear of throwing up every time," Echo replied dryly. Morning sickness had not been kind to her, but it seemed to be ebbing.

"That's good news. I made a vegan version of the pumpkin spice cupcakes, would you like to try one?"

"Can I have coffee with it?" her friend asked hopefully.

"What would your doctor say?" Missy gave her a pointed look.

"My doctor is overly cautious."

"Your doctor is doing what's best for you and your baby. I'll bring you a cupcake and a nice cup of herbal tea, how about that?"

Echo sighed melodramatically. "Fine. You're all in cahoots."

"You betcha," Missy chuckled, heading to the cases for cupcakes. "Is Kel joining us this morning?"

"No, he's at my house, meeting with the realtor."

"He finally convinced you to sell?"

"Well, we're married now, it only makes sense. Besides, his house has a wonderful first floor workshop for me to make my candles in."

Echo owned a candle shop and bookstore which shared an eclectic space in a vintage downtown building. She had started out making candles which smelled like Missy's cupcakes and sold them in the inn and the cupcake shop. They had soon become so popular among tourists and locals alike that she needed to open up her own shop in order to keep up with the demand. When her elderly friend who owned the bookstore next door passed away, she willed the quaint shop to Echo, who opened up the wall between the two spaces, hired a sassy new assistant, and now ran both shops.

"Oh, that's great," Missy exclaimed. "You'll be able to work on your candles while Kel works on his art. How is Scott doing?"

Scott Hammond, a bright fifteen-year-old, was the son that Kel never knew he had until a few weeks ago, when the teenager's mother went missing and was later found murdered. He'd come to live with Kel after his mother disappeared, and was now a delightful addition to the household.

"He's doing well. He misses his mom of course, but he's back in school now and seems to really like it. He's very easy to get along with and is so helpful around the house. I'll miss my cozy little cottage when it sells though," Echo mused.

"How are things going with Petaluma?" Missy asked.

Grayson's alcoholic mother, Petaluma, had come to Florida a week before anyone expected, and had been staying with Echo, who tried to keep the ill-mannered woman out of trouble long enough to see her son get married and return to Louisiana.

"She's utterly infatuated with my neighbor, Steve," Echo sighed, dropping her chin into her hand while she chewed her cupcake.

"Loud Steve?" Missy's eyebrows rose.

The gals had nicknamed Echo's neighbor Steve "Loud Steve" because he had a habit of blasting the music in his pint-sized pickup truck so loudly that one could hear him coming from blocks away. He attempted to flirt with Echo every time he saw her, and was known to sit for hours on end, smoking cigarettes and drinking beer on his front porch while watching Echo's house. The fact that Petaluma had hooked up with the loud, crude neighbor could only mean trouble.

"The one and only," she nodded.

"Oh dear," Missy frowned with worry.

"Yeah, the two of them have been acting like teenagers since Petaluma got here," Echo shook her head. "On the plus side, she seems to have lost all interest in meddling with the details of the wedding."

"Well, that has been nice, but letting her hang out with your neighbor is like throwing her to the wolves. We should try to involve her at least a little bit in the wedding planning. I'm sure Grayson would appreciate it."

"Grayson wasn't even sure that she'd make it to the wedding," Echo pointed out.

"I know, but he only gets married once. Don't you think he'd want us to involve Petaluma? Besides, it's just the right thing to do."

Echo made a face. "I really don't think he'd care, but I suppose you're right. Maybe we can let her tag along when we go to the florist this afternoon."

"Is Joyce going to watch the bookstore and candle shop so that you can leave early?" Missy asked, taking a large sip of piping hot coffee.

"Of course. That girl is a saint, I don't know what I'd do without her."

Joyce Rutledge was a well-educated bookworm who presided over Echo's shops with an eagle eye and an iron will. She knew the answer to every possible literary question that a customer could ask, and was a huge fan of scented candles, making her the perfect employee. She and Echo had become great friends, and Echo had come to rely heavily on the strong, steady presence of the younger woman.

"Great. I'll come by after I close up here. I'll pick you up, then we can swing by your cottage to get Petaluma. We'll wrestle her from Steve's grasp if we have to," Missy's mouth was set in a determined line.

"I'll wait in the car," Echo grumbled. Her phone rang just then. "It's Kel," she explained, answering the call.

Missy discreetly headed toward the kitchen to give the newlyweds privacy for their call, carrying empty plates and mugs with her.

"You're not going to believe this," Echo appeared in the doorway to the kitchen as Missy was loading their dishes into the dishwasher.

"What?" Missy was vaguely alarmed.

"When Kel met the realtor at my cottage a few minutes ago, Petaluma and Steve were… inside," she grimaced. "Apparently they'd been drinking all morning, and were…" she trailed off, shaking her head.

Missy gulped. "They were… ?" her eyes widened.

"Yep, 'fraid so," Echo confirmed, looking disgusted.

"Oh my," Missy covered her mouth with her hands and giggled.

"Not funny," Echo frowned, trying to stifle her own laughter. "I'm going to have to burn that couch," she finally cracked up.

SUMMER PRESCOTT

CHAPTER 2

Missy was glad for the powerful scent of flowers when she, Echo, and Petaluma entered the floral shop to select arrangements for Grayson and Sarah's wedding. After being found in an unwashed and illicit state by Kel and the realtor, Petaluma had spent the afternoon drinking coffee, but still smelled a bit like a distillery. Riding in the car with her had been a rather unpleasant experience that had prompted Echo to lower her window and inhale the warm tropical air, in the interest of holding onto the lunch that she'd consumed hours before.

"Hi, you must be Missy," the lovely young woman behind the counter beamed when they came in.

"And you must be Nari," Missy replied, shaking the pale, slim hand that was offered across the counter.

"Yes, ma'am," she nodded.

Missy introduced Echo and Petaluma, and when Nari found out that Petaluma was the mother of the groom, she gave her a lovely peach-colored rose in full bloom. Echo wondered later if it hadn't been so that the strongly perfumed flower would cover up the scent of stale beer. The three sat down at a round table filled with books of floral arrangements, and Nari began making recommendations based upon conversations that she'd had with Missy.

Acting bored, Petaluma twirled the lovely peach rose round and round, picking the petals off.

"He loves me, he loves me not," she murmured, pulling petal after petal while the other three women stared at her.

"What?" she demanded. "What can I say, I'm in love."

Grayson's mother then finished plucking the remaining petals from the rose, repeating, "he loves me, he loves me not," in a singsong voice, either oblivious to or unconcerned with the looks of alarm from Missy and Echo, and the bemused speculation of Nari.

The young woman's almond-shaped chocolate eyes were warm when Echo mouthed 'sorry' at her, and she waved a hand with an understanding smile.

"Oooh, that one is lovely for the bouquet, and Sarah said that she wanted white roses," Missy exclaimed, determined to move forward with the process, no matter how bizarre Petaluma's behavior might be.

Echo nodded, looking at the page in the book that Nari had marked with a sticky note. "I agree, that is beautiful. Maybe we could add something small and pink, since pink is her wedding party color."

Nari reached into a box behind her chair.

"What do you think of these?" she asked, presenting delicate sprays of tiny pale pink pearls on stems which could be inserted into the bouquet.

"Yes!" Missy and Echo exclaimed together.

"Oh, that'll be elegant," Missy nodded.

Petaluma tossed the stem from her plucked rose aside, muttering, "it don't matter, he loves me anyhow, I know it," and shoved her chair in between Missy and Echo, leaning over to peer at the book.

"Criminy," she breathed, making a face and exhaling something that smelled vaguely like bus fumes. "Did you see how much that thing costs? I could pay rent with that much money. Man, I want a cigarette," she sighed. "So, yeah, there's no way we can do that one," she wrinkled her nose, sat back in her chair and crossed her arms after her pronouncement.

Echo started to open her mouth and Missy reached around Petaluma to squeeze her shoulder, speaking first, before things got ugly.

"Petaluma, honey," Missy began, her southern drawl deepening as it always did when she was stressed. "You don't need to worry about what any of this costs. The wedding is part of our gift to Grayson and Sarah. We'll take care of buying the flowers, and we'll get whatever we think will work. Sarah told me what she wants, and that's all we need to know," she said in a placating voice.

"That's ridiculous. If the bride's family can't pay for stuff, the bride and groom are supposed to do it, and I know that Gray can't afford anything like this," Petaluma scoffed.

Echo saw the look on her friend's face and knew that Missy's blood was beginning to boil, so instead of speaking her mind, which would be her usual choice, she sat back and watched, waiting for Missy's rare temper to show itself.

"What Grayson and Sarah can or cannot afford is not the issue here, and is also not a matter that is up for debate. We're here to select floral arrangements and that's exactly what we're going to do," Missy insisted with a strained smile. Her eyes were tight around the corners, which Echo recognized as a sign of impending doom. She wished she had popcorn.

"Well, who died and made you the Big Kahuna, Miss Thang?" Petaluma challenged, her hangover making her too miserable to hold back. "I say we're gonna get something affordable and I'm Gray's mother, so that's that," she leaned into Missy's face, defiant.

While Missy might have looked outwardly calm to Nari and Petaluma, Echo knew that there might as well be wisps of smoke curling out of the petite blonde's ears. She was gearing up for a whole lot of heavily accented honesty.

"Nari, darlin, would you excuse us for just a moment, honey?" Missy asked sweetly.

"Oh yes, of course," the young woman scurried away, perhaps sensing the imminent storm.

Once she was gone, the smile disappeared from Missy's face and she turned to face Petaluma.

"There's something that you need to understand," she began, her kitten-grey eyes flashing fire. "Grayson is very dear to me, and this wedding is my gift to him. I will see to it that he and Sarah get everything that they want for this wedding, and no one..." she leaned forward in her chair, her nose almost touching Grayson's mother's. "And I absolutely mean No One... is going to stand in the way of their happiness. Am I making myself completely clear here, Petaluma?" she ground out, her teeth clenched, with a savage smile still on her face.

"Just who the heck do you think you are talking to me like that? He's special to you? Well, big whooptie-doo, I'm his mother, how do you like that? I raised that boy, and I have a say in stuff like this, so put that in your hat and smoke it, Missy Prissy."

Echo, wanting to avoid potential disaster, leapt to her feet.

"Missy, can I talk to you outside for a second?" she asked, taking her friend by the shoulders and leading her toward the front door.

"Take your time, I got this," Petaluma called after them. "Hey, girl, where'd you go?"

"I'm here," Nari appeared, as if by magic. "Can I get you something to drink? Some coffee or tea?" she asked, her eyes darting toward the front door, searching for Missy.

Petaluma's eyes narrowed.

"What the heck do you mean by that?" she snarled, advancing toward the soft-spoken young woman. "You trying to say that I need coffee? What did those two tell you about me anyhow?"

"I... no... uh, no one said anything, ma'am. I always offer guests coffee and tea. If you don't like that, I could bring water... or... ?" Nari began apologetically.

"Yeah, sure. You're just like the rest of them, looking down that pretty little nose at drunk old Petaluma. I don't need you to be judging me, you retail-working little..."

"Petaluma!" Missy exclaimed, rushing toward her. "You stop that right now and apologize. Nari has been nothing but nice to all of us, and you can't just throw wild accusations at people," she insisted, her nostrils flaring in a way which signaled to Echo that fireworks might be about to begin.

"I've had just about enough of you hoity-toity types tellin' me what to do and what not to do! You ain't got no right to do that," Grayson's madder-than-a-wet-hen mother squared off with the incensed blonde in front of her. "In fact, I'm done with the lot of ya.

You can take your fancy airs and manners and shove 'em where the sun don't shine. I'm outta here."

With that, she brushed past Missy, her bony shoulder making rough contact with the innkeeper's. Echo placed a warning hand on her friend's arm, whispering in her ear to just let Petaluma go. Missy turned back to an expressionless Nari, shaking with anger, her cheeks burning.

"Nari, I am so sorry…" she began.

"No worries. I work with people in different emotional states… nervous brides, grieving families, husbands who are in the doghouse; you wouldn't believe some of the things I witness on a daily basis," she smiled with understanding. "Would you ladies like a cup of tea?"

"Yes, please," Echo replied with a smile, leading a still-rattled Missy back to the table filled with floral books. "We'll just start looking through these again."

SUMMER PRESCOTT

CHAPTER 3

Izzy Gilmore gazed at the pile of unopened mail on her dining room table and sighed. The world-famous horror author had found herself living in a real-life nightmare when she was abducted a few weeks ago. The works that she penned paled by comparison. After literally losing the tip of her finger in order to escape, she was home now, and safe… as far as she knew. The only thing that she knew about her captor was that he had come to her looking for her ex-boyfriend, a Marine veteran named Spencer Bengal. Where Spencer was, and why the awful man who'd taken her was looking for him was a mystery.

Izzy had replaced her cell phone when she'd returned to her pretty pink cottage in Calgon. Her old phone had gone missing when she was abducted, and the new device had immediately starting pinging with notifications of texts, voicemails, and emails, nearly all from her overbearing publisher, wondering why she'd missed the deadline for her latest book.

"How sad is it that I get kidnapped for a few weeks, and when I come home, the only messages I have are from my publisher?" the depressed young author murmured, turning off the notification sounds on her phone and tossing it onto the table.

The mail would wait, her book would wait, all she could think of at the moment was a hot bath and a sandwich. Certain that everything in her fridge had spoiled, she made a mental note to order the sandwich for delivery when she got out of the tub, and trudged upstairs.

Easing into the steaming, fragrant water, Izzy made certain that the bandage wrapped around the end of her abbreviated finger didn't get wet. She had no idea how she was going to become accustomed to typing without her pinkie fingertip, but she knew she didn't really have a choice, so she'd figure it out somehow. Life seemed so bleak at the moment. Spencer had finally poured out his heart to her, ready to commit, and she'd turned him away. There was just too much about him that she didn't understand, and wasn't sure that she wanted to understand. He was sweet and kind and handsome and everything she'd ever wanted in a man, but she just couldn't deal with the secrets of his past and present, and she'd told him so. The crushed look in his eyes had practically torn her heart from her chest, but she'd remained steadfast in her resolve, which left her here, hurting and alone.

Her doorbell rang, and she ignored it. She hadn't ordered her sandwich yet, so there was no reason that anyone should be ringing the bell. Whoever was at the door rang the bell one more time, and knocked for good measure, then gave up, much to Izzy's relief. She wasn't up to dealing with people right now, particularly because the last time she'd answered her door she'd been abducted.

She was rewrapping her stitched-up finger, which had actually given her the inspiration for a hospital scene in her latest book, when she cocked her head to the side, listening. Had she heard something? Was it her imagination running wild? PTSD? Her heart sped up, and she held her breath, silently setting down the adhesive tape that she'd been using. Izzy waited, breathing shallowly and listening hard, for several minutes before deciding that she was just being paranoid. While it was true that she had good reason to be more than a bit afraid, after having been kidnapped from her own home, she had to realize that the odds of something like that happening to the same person twice within a month were astronomically in her favor.

Giving herself a shake, Izzy pulled on a pair of yoga pants and a comfy, shapeless t-shirt. She didn't really care how she looked at this point. After she finished her sandwich, she planned to hole up and write for as many hours as she could before sleep claimed her. Running a hand through her hair, giving the damp locks a little toss to help them dry, the author looked at herself in the mirror, gave a resigned sigh upon spotting the suitcases below her eyes, and headed for the stairs.

She dialed the number to the deli from memory, and nearly dropped her phone when she walked into the living room and saw two dark, menacing-looking men sitting casually in her floral chintz chairs as though they'd dropped in for a spot of tea. She hung up on the deli and stared at the men, more angry than frightened.

"What now?" she demanded, crossing her arms defiantly. "Are you here to kidnap me too?" she asked, when the men didn't respond.

Izzy didn't drop her gaze, refusing to budge. She wouldn't speak again until they had. Her heart was thudding in her chest and adrenalin raced through her veins, but her anger kept her strong, and she gritted her teeth, determined to wait them out.

"Where is Steve Arnold?" one of them asked, finally, in a heavily accented voice.

"Who is Steve Arnold?" her eyes narrowed.

"We don't have time to play games," the other goon growled with an equally heavy accent.

"Well, that's just dandy," Izzy raised her voice, furious. "Because I don't have time for this stupid harassment either. I have no idea who you're talking about, and you can just take your attitude and get out," she shouted, heading for the door.

One of the men appeared between her and the door in a flash.

"Great, a ninja," the exasperated author muttered, glad that at least the man hadn't touched her… yet.

"It is very important that we… speak to him immediately," the man in front of her insisted in a low voice.

She noted the holstered weapons crossed over the man's chest, and the bulge near his ankle, and swallowed hard. Bravely holding eye contact, she took a deep breath and let it out in a sigh.

"Look, I really have no idea what you're talking about," she shook her head, cursing the fact that she had very little recollection of what had happened to her when she'd been kidnapped, other than that she had sacrificed part of her pinkie to escape.

The man reached into his back pocket and Izzy winced, hoping that he wasn't drawing a gun. He pulled out a photo that made Izzy's heart drop to her knees. In the photo were three men, Spencer, the man who had helped him rescue her, and the man who had kidnapped her. The photo was dark and looked like it had been taken a few years earlier. Spencer looked younger than she had ever seen him, and had short hair rather than his long dark waves.

"Do you know these men?" he demanded, shoving the picture at her.

Izzy's mind raced. She didn't want to admit to knowing Spencer, thinking that it might somehow put him in danger, but she wanted to give the men something that would make them go away.

"The one in the middle kidnapped me a few weeks ago," she admitted, wrapping her arms around her midsection and dropping her gaze.

"Where did he take you?" the other man barked, coming over to stand beside the first one.

"I have no idea. I was blindfolded and drugged. I remember being on an airplane, and waking up on a beach a few miles from here a few days ago," she lied, her voice trembling.

"Were you kept in a cell?"

"No, I don't think so. It sounded like I was in a city. I heard sirens and cars outside and kept hoping that someone would come rescue me."

The two men exchanged a glance and seemed to come to some sort of decision. To Izzy's profound relief, they moved toward her kitchen, heading for the back door. With one hand on the knob, the first man turned around and gave Izzy a look that sent chills down her spine.

"If you are lying, it will not go well for you. Whatever Steve Arnold did will seem like child's play when we are done with you," he promised darkly.

Izzy stared at them wordlessly as they slipped out the door, refusing to be intimidated. When they left, closing the door quietly behind them, she nearly fainted with relief, but was terrified at their parting statement. She'd been lying like crazy and now wondered what on earth she should do. Thinking for a moment, she dialed the number for Detective Chas Beckett.

SUMMER PRESCOTT

CHAPTER 4

D etective Chas Beckett picked up his desk phone. It never rained but it poured. He'd just gotten a call that a homicide victim, had been discovered in a public restroom at the beach, and now, the desk sergeant had buzzed him letting him know that he had an urgent caller on the line.

"Beckett," he spoke into the receiver, trying to keep the annoyance out of his voice. "When did they leave?" he asked in a gentler tone, after listening to Izzy Gilmore at length. "Have you touched the doorknob since they left? Good, don't touch it. I'll send a forensics guy out as soon as I can. Are you safe? Okay, just try to relax. I'll have a patrol car stop by, and…"

Chas was interrupted by a very vehement Izzy at that point.

"Oh, I see," he replied gravely, closing his eyes for a brief moment. "Okay, well, sit tight then. I'll make certain that the forensics guy arrives in an unmarked car, then I'll come over to take a statement myself, but it may not be until later this afternoon. Something… came up."

When the detective hung up the phone, he was deeply troubled, and couldn't help but wonder if the body found on the beach had anything to do with the visit that Izzy had received from the two strange men with heavy accents. He glanced down at his desk calendar, not surprised at all to see that it was Monday, then grabbed his keys and headed for the door.

***

"Hey Timmy," Fiona McCammish, Mortuary Manager, poked her head into her boss, Timothy Eckels' office. "We got another stiff."

"Don't call me that," the mild-mannered mortician and coroner replied automatically, but he looked up with interest. "Cause of death?"

"It was the homicide guy who called," Fiona tried not to smile.

The quirky young woman, whom Tim had required to get a makeover before he'd hire her, was fascinated with both the forensics and body preparation aspects of her job. The formerly pierced and mohawked gal was the perfect choice for Tim's assistant. She was bold and brash, where he was introverted to the extreme. She was attractive and personable, while he was doughy and pale, sporting thick, nerdy glasses. Fiona handled the "people" side of the mortuary business: sales, funerals, wakes, etc.… while Tim taught the investigation and preparation techniques which fascinated her to no end.

"Address?" he rose from his chair.

"Already plugged into GPS," she replied, going through the familiar ritual.

"My bag?" he led the way to the mortuary's garage.

"Already in the car. I'm driving."

"No, you're not."

"You're no fun," she pretended to pout.

"I'm aware."

***

Even Fiona sobered when she saw the victim splayed out on the sandy bathroom floor in a puddle of blood.

"Wow, she looks so beautiful, like a porcelain doll," she whispered as her boss stepped carefully around the body, taking photos at multiple angles.

"Push the hair back from her neck," Tim instructed, focused on his task.

Fiona reached a gloved hand down, and without disturbing the body, pushed aside the young woman's thick, shiny black hair.

"Ah, ligature," she murmured, noting the bruises. "But why would someone strangle her and then stab her too?"

Tim's response was to glance at her briefly with an eyebrow raised. She'd done it again. She knew that her boss didn't like her speculating about the victim, or discussing details at the crime scene. He never made assumptions and refused to provide theories until after he'd had a chance to do a thorough examination.

The coroner finished taking photos of the victim and the scene, then, with Fiona's assistance, he bagged up the young woman's body and loaded it into the hearse, making his way to the county morgue. He spent most of his time running the mortuary that he owned, but did double duty as the county coroner when he was needed, so he had offices both in the mortuary and the morgue. Fiona was paid to assist Tim in the mortuary, but chose to hang out with him and learn on her own time at the morgue. As long as she didn't distract him from his tasks, he indulged the young woman's interest in autopsies and asked her to assist on occasion.

"So why would someone strangle her and then stab her?" she asked the moment they climbed into the car to transport the body.

Tim grimaced and sighed, clearly he was uncomfortable with the subject, which surprised his assistant. The man was typically unflappable when it came to even the most dastardly homicides.

"There are a couple of common possibilities… her attacker could have strangled her just long enough for her to lose consciousness so that they could transport her somewhere else, or…" he swallowed and trailed off.

"Or what?" Fiona prompted sitting forward in her seat.

Tim sighed again.

"Sometimes these things can be… sexual in nature," he replied, eyes straight ahead, corners of his mouth turned down.

Fiona's eyes grew wide.

"Oh, duh. Of course, why didn't I think of that?" she nodded. "She didn't look like the sex game type though."

"Never judge a book by its cover. We'll know soon enough. Clearly the strangulation didn't kill the victim. We'll look for other clues during the autopsy."

"Oh, I never judge. For all I know, you could be one of those people who likes to get their freak on," she teased, knowing she'd get a reaction from her boss.

"Don't be preposterous," Tim kept his eyes forward, gazing out at the traffic through coke-bottle thick lenses, and it looked like his grip on the steering wheel might have tightened a tiny bit. "That's entirely inappropriate."

"Oh lighten up, Timmy," she grinned, full of mischief and knowing that he'd soon forgive and forget the awkward conversation. "It's not like you have an HR department to report me to."

The mortician didn't dignify her comment with a reply.

***

"You're certain that one of the men touched the doorknob and didn't have gloves on?" Chas stared at an extremely shaken Izzy Gilmore.

"Yes, I watched him. Why?"

"The forensics tech didn't find any trace of fingerprints. Not even a partial."

"How is that possible? That just doesn't make sense. I saw him open the door with his bare hand," Izzy shook her head.

Chas had an idea of what might have happened, and he seriously hoped, for Izzy's sake, that he was wrong. If no fingerprints showed up, it may be that the gentlemen who had paid her a visit didn't have fingerprints, which would mean that they were professionals, and the implications of that could be dire. Izzy had told the detective everything, from beginning to end, begging him to not go through official channels to investigate, because she feared for Spencer's safety if the goons who had shown up knew that she had gone to the police.

Chas took descriptions of Steve Arnold, and of the two men, and promised her that he'd be discreet in his investigation.

"Is there anyone that you can stay with? Your safety may be at risk," he warned the weary author.

"I think that my safety would be at risk no matter where I go, so I'm just going to batten down the hatches and hope for the best," Izzy sighed.

"I'll send some unmarked cars on periodic drive-bys. If you get scared, don't hesitate to call, and don't be afraid to use my cell number," the detective instructed.

"Thanks," Izzy shook his hand and led him to the door, determined to disappear into her work, where the deliberate horror was far less scary than her present situation.

SUMMER PRESCOTT

CHAPTER 5

Spencer Bengal was staring into his beer at a dive bar in a tiny town in Idaho when the text tone on his phone buzzed his pocket. No one knew where he was, and there shouldn't have been anyone trying to get in touch with him, but he reached into the pocket of his well-worn jeans anyway. The text consisted simply of a number... a number that he knew only too well. He downed his beer in a series of quick gulps, left a bill on the counter for the bartender, and headed for the local outfitter.

In a matter of minutes the Marine had what he needed. He paid for his purchases in cash, much to the astonishment of the proprietor, who typically only sold some fishing lures and hunting knives on any given day. The transaction represented such a windfall for him that he closed up early after Spencer left, and headed for the barstool that the Marine had just vacated.

Night vision goggles would make getting through the woods easier, and Spencer preferred to travel under the cover of darkness. The code that he'd received could only mean trouble, and he wanted to slip into his destination undetected, assessing the lay of the land before deciding on his next move. His mind was focused fully on the task at hand. When he'd been mulling over his beer, his thoughts had been consumed with Izzy, the woman who had refused his love, twice. He missed her, but understood her reluctance to get involved with someone whose associations had already gotten her kidnapped.

Spencer Bengal was a man on a mission. His fellow Marine, Janssen, who was like a brother to him, had sent out a distress call, and he would answer it. The last time he'd heard from his war-scarred friend, he'd been taking Izzy's kidnapper to a place where he wouldn't be hurting anyone anymore. Spencer and Janssen had served in a very special capacity in the military, and had participated in a program where their former identities had been erased, in the interest of national security.

Steve Arnold, the man who had kidnapped Izzy in hopes of using her as leverage to bring Spencer and Janssen in, had been tasked with keeping track of them in case their country needed them to serve in a mission that most wouldn't be coming back from. The contract that the young men had signed with the government had ended, but that didn't stop their former unit, known simply as "Command," from searching for them when special missions needed to be done. Spencer and Janssen had both gone underground in their own ways, to avoid being sent out into another hellish war zone, but Steve had managed to track them down and had been making their lives difficult for close to a year now.

Spencer had settled into a job, posing as a handyman at the bed and breakfast inn that Chas and Missy owned, but in reality, he'd been hired fresh out of the military by Chas's late father's manservant, Chalmers, to provide security for Chas, who was the eldest heir to the Beckett fortune. When Chas had declined to manage his family business, preferring to serve his fellow man in law enforcement, his father had made certain that he was guarded twenty-four hours a day. Spencer had followed the detective's every move for years, making certain that no harm came to him. Once he seemed to have shaken the government from his tail, he became more relaxed, actually applying for a job at the inn, so that he could observe the Beckett family more closely.

Janssen, who sported a dramatic facial scar, had never been able to assimilate back into civilian life after having been witness to and participant in so many war-time blood-baths, had shadowed Spencer wherever he went, living off the land, staying hidden, but close enough to help out if necessary. There had been some close calls over the years, but the two of them always managed to do what needed to be done to keep Chas and Missy safe.

When the two Marines last parted, Spencer had taken Izzy to the airport after rescuing her from Steve Arnold, and Janssen had taken Steve back to the cell where Izzy had been confined. Spencer had suggested to Janssen that Steve should be left alive if at all possible, but he had no idea what had happened after leaving them, and now he'd received the distress call. He hoped that Steve hadn't somehow turned the tables on his buddy, and was on his way to make sure.

According to the coordinates that he'd received, he'd have a day and a half of jogging through the woods in order to reach the confinement facility. He'd travel at night, and find a safe place in the woods to sleep before approaching the facility. He wanted to be fresh, with all of his wits about him. The Marine was well armed, but would only use his weapons as a last resort. A gunshot in the middle of the wilderness could bring all kinds of unwanted attention, and stealth was his best friend at the moment.

Spencer moved lightly and swiftly through the trees, falling into a steady, easy rhythm that ate up the miles, while still being cautious enough to not trip over brush, stumps, and roots. As daylight approached, he found an area between two rocks that would shield him from sight and settled in for a nap, pulling brush and branches across the opening between the rocks to further camouflage himself. Backpack behind his head, he slept sitting up, one hand on his hunting knife.

Hours of daylight had passed when the Marine awoke abruptly, his expert senses alerting him to the fact that he wasn't alone. Motionless, he opened his eyes and listened hard, hearing nothing, but unable to shake the feeling that something, or someone, was nearby. The grip on his knife tightened imperceptibly as he readied himself to spring into action if necessary. He was puzzled, any woodland creature would surely have given away its position by now, but Spencer hadn't even heard a leaf rustle or a twig snap.

"Just keep that pig-sticker in its sheath, boy, I ain't gonna hurt ya," a vaguely familiar voice drawled.

Spencer rose to his feet, his hand securely on the knife, and peered through the brush in front of his hiding spot. In front of him was Norm, the mountain man who'd found Izzy nearly dead in the woods after she had escaped from Steve Arnold. He'd made a stretcher and transported her back to his cabin, treating her with folk remedies as she battled infection and dehydration. The rough-looking but kind hermit regarded the Marine with an open, friendly demeanor.

"Norm?" he asked, not quite knowing what to say, and unaccustomed to being spotted when he didn't want to be.

"Yep," the mountain man nodded. "I remember you. Things work out with that pretty little gal?" he asked mildly, not intimidated in the least by the powerful and well-armed man in front of him.

"In a manner of speaking," Spencer muttered, kicking himself for not being more careful about his cover.

"I'm heading to my place to grab some food if you're needing lunch. You're welcome to join. Ain't nobody out here but you, me and the critters right now."

Spencer considered his options. There were hours of daylight left, and he didn't want to travel until at least dusk, so holing up in the hermit's cabin might not be a bad way to pass the afternoon.

"Sounds good," he nodded at last. "How did you know I was here?" the Marine asked as he followed Norm's lead back to the cabin.

"Son, I know these woods like the back of my hand. That spot you were sleepin' in was one that I use for trappin' smaller critters sometimes. I saw that the brush around it looked different and came over to take a look. You look like a man who don't want to be found, but don't worry none, ain't nobody out here but me, and any others who mighta happened by wouldn't have seen ya. I just knew what to look fer."

Spencer felt a bit better after the reassurance, knowing that Norm had special knowledge and skills that the average operative wouldn't have, but he still made a mental note to be more careful. The two men moved silently through the trees until they reached Norm's cabin. Once inside, the mountain man set about making lunch, clanging cast iron pans, dicing potatoes and slicing thick slabs of meat.

"I s'pose you're looking for them two fellas who came around here a few days ago," Norm remarked casually, putting Spencer on instant alert.

"Two men? Who were they?" he asked, staring hard at the mountain man. "Were they the men that I came here with originally?" he asked, referring to when he, Janssen, and Steve Arnold had tracked Izzy down.

Norm shook his head, cracking some eggs into a pan.

"Nope, dark fellas. They weren't from here, talked kinda funny."

"You spoke with them?"

"Nope, they didn't even know I was trackin' 'em. I just wanted to make sure that they didn't come near my cabin."

"Which way were they headed?"

"Same way you came from last time."

Spencer's mind raced. It sounded as though there had been foreign operatives heading toward the confinement facility, which could explain why Janssen had sent the distress call.

"There were only two of them?" he confirmed.

"Yup, and they moved real quiet. They weren't country boys, but they knew how to leave no trace, that's fer sure."

A tingle of worry curled at the bottom of the Marine's spine. Professionals. But who would be coming after Janssen and Steve? Or did the two strangers just happen to be in the area because they were looking for something or someone else at the facility? Spencer was anxious to get back on the trail, but now knew that it was more important than ever to travel under the cover of darkness, despite the urgency that gripped him. He hoped that he wasn't already too late. There were at least two men that he'd have to deal with, so he'd plan accordingly.

"I expect you'll be wanting to lay low 'til around sundown," Norm commented, sliding eggs out of the pan and onto a plate.

"If that's all right with you," Spencer nodded grimly.

"Fine by me. You can get a good meal in ya before gettin' on yer way."

"I appreciate it."

"Them two fellas had quite the arsenal between 'em. I'd be a mite careful if I was you," the mountain man cautioned.

"I intend to be."

***

Spencer Bengal lay flat, his body no more than a shadow in the cloudy evening. He was perched on a berm which surrounded the confinement facility, gazing down into the squat grey building with night vision magnification lenses. He hadn't seen any movement, but he knew that there were people inside because some rooms were lit, and the red lights atop the security cameras blinked balefully, taking in the entirety of the area.

The Marine scanned the area, looking for a way to get past the cameras, and knowing that there wasn't going to be an easy way to slip past. His eyes traveled over the building, exploring various routes in, but each one was covered by multiple cameras. Sighing inwardly, his eyes raised to the roof. There were no cameras up there, the area was completely unwatched, so if he could figure out a way to enter the complex from above, he'd be able to drop in wherever he wanted. Even more importantly, once he had access to the ductwork which ran throughout the complex, he'd be able to position himself to disable security systems and gain easier access.

The facility had a guard tower in one corner of the property, which was unmanned at the moment. The tower faced the part of the building that housed a backup generator and multiple cooling units, so there were no windows on that side. Spencer visually measured the distance and determined that if he could get up into the tower, he'd be able to run a zip line from the tower to the roof on the utility side of the building and enter that way. The tower was on the opposite corner of the property from where he lay, and there were only a few hours of darkness left, so he'd have to run through the woods, skirting the property line, to get to the other side in time to make his move.

Gathering his gear, he slipped down the back of the berm and disappeared into the woods like a shadow, headed for the guard tower. The Marine moved swiftly and stealthily until he made it to the treeline directly behind the guard tower. He was still nearly fifty feet short of the guard tower, and couldn't make it across the swath of grass in order to get there undetected. Catching his breath, Spencer leaned against a gently swaying evergreen behind him, the fragrance of its boughs filling the air with a delightful scent.

Craning his head upward to gaze at the dark clumps of needles above him, he was struck with an idea. The beautiful tree rose to a height of nearly seventy feet. The closest branch to the ground was about a foot and a half over his head, and he jumped up to test it, backpack and all, catching his weight with both hands. The branch didn't even creak and certainly didn't budge under his weight. Decision made, Spencer moved steadily upward, his hands coated with sticky, fragrant pitch. As he neared the top of the mighty evergreen, he tested the branches for flexibility and found them to be more than pliable, which would make his plan work perfectly... with a little luck.

Climbing until he was a mere ten feet from the top of the gently swaying tree, the Marine felt a bit of vertigo and reminded himself not to look down. If he fell from this height, even with branches breaking his fall, he probably wouldn't walk away from it, and he couldn't afford to make that kind of mistake, Janssen needed his help.

There was a glassless window in the tower wall that faced him, and a ledge right below it. Spencer's plan was to inch his way toward the top of the tree, bending the tip of it toward the guard tower until he was close enough to jump. He'd grab onto the window ledge with his hands and swing his feet up onto the ledge, allowing him to climb into the window so that he could set up the zip line to the utility wall. He'd either make it or die trying, and he had no plans to let Janssen down, so he set his mouth in a determined line and climbed upward, feeling each branch for strength and flexibility as he went.

As the Marine neared the top, the mammoth tree began to shudder under his weight. Heart in his throat, he stopped until the shaking stopped. If the top of the tree snapped, he'd go down with it, to his peril.

And down will come baby, cradle and all...

The nursery rhyme sing-songed through his mind like a premonition of doom, but he ignored it and continued to climb, only pausing when he heard creaks beneath his hands or feet. When he reached the top of the tree, it trembled without ceasing, and he seriously hoped that no one decided to take a walk outside. He hadn't come this far to be caught like a treed animal. He put his hand just a few feet from the tip of the tree, and the trunk bowed toward the tower like he'd hoped it would, but it stopped several feet short of his target.

Taking a deep breath, Spencer began to rhythmically swing his feet back and forth, the top of the tree dipping lower and closer to the tower with each swing. When he was nearly close enough to the tower to reach out and touch it, he heard a groan and a small crunching sound, and he dropped a few inches all at once. Glancing back at where the tree was bent at nearly a ninety degree angle, he saw the trunk beginning to splinter. He didn't have much time. He heard another crack and knew that it was do or die, literally. Taking a deep breath, he swung his body hard toward the tower and let go of the tree. The trunk snapped back most of the way, dangling at a slight angle toward the tower, and Spencer hit the concrete blocks in front of him hard enough to jar his teeth. He reached desperately for the window ledge with both hands, but his right hand missed, leaving him dangling by his left.

Heart slamming in his chest, he felt the rough edge of the concrete window cutting into the skin behind his second knuckles and abrading his palms. His feet scrabbled, missing the ledge, and his fingers started to slip from the window. With a Herculean effort, he gritted his teeth and dug his fingertips, now bloody, into the ledge, swinging his right hand up and making contact. Once his right hand held him more securely, his feet found purchase on the ledge, and he was able to rest for a moment, catching his breath. Spencer froze in place, listening for any sound outside which would indicate that he'd been spotted, hearing nothing but night sounds all around.

His left hand throbbing, he used his legs to propel himself upward, bringing his arms over the ledge and into the window, hanging by his underarms. Inching to the side, he swung his leg up to the window, catching the ledge with his ankle and pulling himself up and in. He was bruised, scraped, and his left hand was a bit worse for wear, but he'd made it inside, and his battle for entry was only half finished.

Crouching low, he moved across the guard tower to the window which faced the utility wall. Sliding up the wall beside the window, he looked out, seeing no one. Still confident that he'd gone undetected as yet, he surveyed the facility below him and formulated the next step to his plan. Spencer felt the intruder in the room a mere split second before he felt the cold barrel of a gun against his temple.

SUMMER PRESCOTT

CHAPTER 6

"She wasn't killed in the bathroom," Timothy Eckels mused, gazing at the photos of the crime scene.

"How do you know that?" Fiona asked, peering over his shoulder in a manner that she knew irritated him.

"There wasn't nearly enough blood at the scene, there were no spatter marks on the walls or any other surfaces, and there was no trace of the murder weapon. Also, look over there, by the door... see the pattern in the sand?" Tim pointed with a gloved finger.

"Yeah, so?" she frowned.

Tim sighed and raised an eyebrow at his assistant.

"It's a drag pattern, see the sweeps?" he jabbed his finger at the photo again.

Fiona's eyes brightened. "Oh, duh! Of course, yeah, I see it now," she nodded.

"Beckett probably already picked up on that, but go give him a call, just in case."

Fiona scurried off to call the detective, and Tim continued to scan the photos before beginning the autopsy. He'd taken scrapings from beneath the young woman's nails, and had sent her clothing in for analysis of tiny blood spatters that he'd detected. There were also hair samples on her clothing which clearly didn't belong to her, and he'd bagged those as well.

***

The young victim's mother and stepfather had already given Detective Chas Beckett permission to search her room for possible clues, and he was standing in the very pink and feminine bedroom when he received the call from Fiona McCammish. He thanked her for the call, and hung up quickly, focusing on the victim's room. It was in perfect condition… too perfect. Everything was neat, tidy, and in its place, which seemed a bit unusual for someone who was still young enough to be living at home while going to college. There wasn't even a speck of dust anywhere, and the bed was perfectly made. Chas went into the living room for a moment, where the young woman's mother and stepfather huddled together on the couch, hands wrapped around mugs of tea.

"Mrs. Lee, do you have a housekeeper?" he asked the petite woman, whose brow seemed to be permanently creased with grief.

"No, I clean my own home," she replied softly.

"Do you clean your daughter's room?" Chas continued, sitting across from the couple in an easy chair.

She shook her head.

"No, I usually just tell her to shut her door so that I don't have to see the room," was the sad, fond reply.

"She tended to be a bit messy?"

"Oh yes, she's young and has her mind on other things," the grieving mother gave a crooked half-smile.

"I'd like to bring a team in here to look around and see if we can come up with any clues that she may have left in her room. Would that be okay with you?" the detective asked gently, his eyes warm.

Mrs. Lee looked at her husband, who nodded slowly.

"Of course," Mr. Lee replied, taking his wife's hand. "What would you be looking for? We'd like to preserve her room just the way that she left it, if you don't mind."

"We'd make sure to leave it as we found it, as much as possible," Chas assured them. "Sometimes young women leave clues to what's going on in their lives without even realizing it. Did your daughter have a boyfriend?"

Mr. Lee's face tightened into a scowl.

"She had an ex-boyfriend that we did not approve of in the least."

"Oh? Can you tell me more about him?"

Mrs. Lee set her mug of tea down on the glass-topped coffee table and shook her head.

"Logan ran with a bad crowd. His father is well respected, so he managed to avoid getting into any serious trouble, but he was just… wild. They'd had a fight recently, so we don't know if they were still together or not."

"What's Logan's last name?"

"Greitzer. Logan Greitzer," Mr. Lee supplied, sounding bitter.

"Councilman Greitzer's son?" the detective guessed.

"Yes, his father pulled strings to keep him out of trouble."

"I'll talk to him. Do you know if your daughter had any enemies?"

Mrs. Lee's eyes filled with tears and she clutched at her husband's hand before replying.

"I don't know how she could've had any enemies… everyone loved her. She was sweet and kind and beautiful. She'd help anyone who needed it… this is so senseless," she exclaimed, bursting into tears and burying her face in her husband's shoulder.

Chas gazed at the couple with compassion, then spoke to Mr. Lee as he comforted his distraught wife.

"We're going to have a team working in the house for quite a while. We'll be in and out, and I'm sorry to inconvenience you, but if you'd like to go stay with friends or family for a day or two while we check things out, that's completely understandable."

"We were thinking of going away for a few days before all of this happened, maybe we should just do that, so that you have room to work without us being in the way," Mr. Lee murmured, stroking his wife's hair.

"That would be fine. I can take your contact information and notify you if we come up with any leads in the case," Chas reassured them.

"Okay. Bring in your team, we'll be gone in an hour."

***

Logan Greitzer lounged indolently on a leather sectional, popping pizza rolls into his mouth while watching TV and flipping through social media sites on his phone. He didn't even look up when his mother, Leasa, came into the room, followed by Detective Chas Beckett.

"Logan, can you turn that off please?" she asked, her face tight.

Still not looking up from his phone, Logan reached over to the remote and hit the power button with his thumb, leaving a greasy print.

Seeming embarrassed, his mother addressed him again.

"Logan, Detective Beckett is here to see you," she cleared her throat and crossed her arms.

The young man fished another pizza roll out of the fine china bowl and tossed it in his mouth, finally looking up from his phone.

"Whazzup?" he drawled, clearly disinterested.

"Where were you yesterday between the hours of one and four this morning?" Chas asked, noting that Logan was clearly not intimidated by his presence.

"Why?" was the bored response, as the young man chewed his food.

"Well, he was here of course," Leasa broke in. "That's the middle of the night... where else would he have been. I'm sure he'd been asleep for hours by then, right Logan?"

"Sure," he shrugged, going back to social media.

"Is that true? Were you here during those hours?" Chas persisted.

"Just like the lady said," Logan smirked, glancing up briefly from his phone.

"Can you prove that?"

"Prove what? That I was asleep?" the young man scoffed, rolling his eyes.

"When is the last time that you saw Nari Lee?"

Logan tossed his phone down and sighed in annoyance.

"A few days ago… I don't know, why?"

"She was murdered this morning, and I'm hoping you might have some insight into who might want to kill an innocent young woman," the detective moved closer. "Do you have any insight that you can lend to the investigation, Logan?" he asked, staring him down.

"Murdered? That's crazy. She could be a high-maintenance pain, but I can't think of anyone who'd want to kill her," he shrugged, seemingly unaffected.

"I heard that the two of you had a disagreement recently…" Chas began, and Logan expelled a breath, clearly offended.

"Dude, don't even go there. That's just dumb. Yeah, we had an argument, we argued all the time… she thrived on it."

"What was the nature of the argument, and when did you have it?"

"No idea, it's not like I kept track of that stuff."

Logan stuffed the last three pizza rolls into his mouth, picked up his bowl and headed for the kitchen.

"Logan?" his mother called after him, blushing and looking worried.

"We're done here," he replied without turning around, the pizza rolls making his words hard to distinguish. "Have a nice day, Detective."

SUMMER PRESCOTT

CHAPTER 7

P etaluma held her hands out to both sides, steadying herself and trying to figure out why the room always seemed to move when she stood up. She and Steve had been having a grand old time in his living room, talking like they'd known each other forever, and somehow, without either of them really noticing it, the twelve pack of beer that they'd started at breakfast had disappeared. She'd tell Steve to take a look at his floors this afternoon, maybe after they napped a bit, something clearly had to be done about the unsteadiness in the house, but for now, food was on her mind, and while Steve stared at the television, she headed to the kitchen in search of leftovers in the nearly empty fridge.

She frowned when the doorbell rang, because the awful sound made her head throb. And when her head throbbed, her stomach swam, again reminding her of the urgent need for food.

"Get it," Steve hollered from the couch.

"You get it, it ain't my house," Petaluma replied crossly.

"Earn your keep, woman," he cackled, only half-kidding.

"I'll toss one of them beer cans at your head, fool," she replied, maintaining her course toward the fridge.

"Fine, you ornery girl," Steve sighed, still smiling.

He lurched up from the threadbare couch and lumbered toward the door just as the bell rang again.

"I'm comin, I'm comin," he grumbled, just as whoever was on the other side started rapping loudly, using the rusted gargoyle door knocker. "Dang, hold your horses, I said I'm comin," he hollered, pressing his hands to his temples when the action shot daggers through his muddled brain.

"What?" he demanded, flinging the door open.

"I'm here to see Petaluma Myers," Jeong Lee demanded, nostrils flaring.

"Pet, did you order take-out?" Steve called back into the house. He turned back to Mr. Lee. "Hang on, man, I'll go get her, I ain't got no money."

Closing the door on the seething Mr. Lee, he went back into the house and found Petaluma sitting on the kitchen floor, eating months-old ice cream from a carton with a serving spoon.

"Don't eat that nasty stuff, Beautiful, the dude from the take-out place is at the door," he smiled, helping her to her feet as best he could. They both swayed a bit and she planted a gooey, ice cream kiss on his cheek.

"You ordered take-out for me?" she cooed, twining her fingers in his beard.

"Nope, you ordered it, he asked for you."

"I didn't order it," Petaluma frowned.

"You probably just forgot," Steve grinned down at her. "Go get some money and get our food. I'll wait for you in the living room," he instructed, just as Jeong Lee knocked again, loudly. "Hold your water, dude, she's comin, jeez!" he yelled before plopping back down on the couch, making sure to avoid the spring that had come up between the cushions.

Petaluma pawed through her purse, coming up with a few bills and a handful of change.

"I hope this'll cover it," she slurred, holding the money out to Nari's irate stepfather. "It's all I got."

Mr. Lee glanced down at the money with contempt.

"You killed my daughter," he snarled.

Petaluma stared at him open-mouthed. "Huh?" was all she could come up with in response to his accusation.

"I saw the video. You screamed at my daughter, you acted violently toward her, and I know it was you who killed her," he growled.

"Now just what in the Sam Heck is going on out here? Where's the food?" Steve blustered, confused when he came to investigate the raised voices.

"I'm taking you to the police," Jeong threatened Petaluma, ignoring Steve.

"Oh no, you ain't," she found her voice. "I'm out of here," the still-drunk woman raised the palm of her hand inches from Lee's nose and turned on her heel.

Jeong Lee grabbed her by the shoulder, accidentally catching her hair as she pulled away and ran down the hall.

"Ow, that hurt, you dirtbag!" she yelled, patting her head. "You just better get on outta here before my boyfriend makes mincemeat outta you," Petaluma threatened, as Steve stood blocking Lee from entering the house.

"This isn't over," Lee's voice was shaking. "You're going to pay for this."

"Hit the road, buddy. I'm a trained veteran and I'd hate to have to take you down," Steve stepped toward the furious stepfather, not quite certain what was happening, but feeling like his girlfriend's knight in shining armor nonetheless.

"You're going to jail," Jeong pointed a shaking finger at Petaluma before slowly backing away from the door.

Steve slammed it shut and turned to Petaluma. "So what about the dang food?"

***

Echo rushed in to Cupcakes in Paradise, as pale as a ghost.

"Hey darlin," Missy greeted her, heading behind the counter for vegan cupcakes. "Oh no, what's wrong?" she asked, seeing the look on her best friend's face.

"A girl was murdered early this morning," Echo sank into a bistro chair, seeming dazed.

"Yeah, I heard. Chas got called early," Missy sat down across from her, concerned. "Did you know her?"

"We both knew her... it was Nari, from the floral shop."

"What?" Missy was astounded. "Why on earth would someone want to murder a sweet young girl like Nari? Was it a robbery?"

Echo shook her head. "It couldn't have been, her body was found in a public bathroom at one of the beaches."

"Oh how awful! How did you find out?"

"It was on the news at noon. They don't have any suspects yet... it's just terrible."

"That poor girl, I feel so bad. She was so helpful and full of life," Missy murmured.

"I know, it was like she really cared about Grayson's wedding."

Missy's phone rang just then, and she pulled it out of the pocket of her jeans.

"Speaking of Grayson," she commented, showing Echo the caller ID before taking the call. "Maybe he's heard some good news about Sarah, maybe she's home."

"Hey sugar," she answered, trying to sound positive after the dreadful news that she'd just heard.

Missy talked to Grayson for a few minutes, learning that he'd found a few of his fiancée's personal items missing from her apartment. They were not things that anyone would typically steal, but things that made it seem as though perhaps she'd gone away for a few days.

"Grayson, honey, listen… I think I know where Sarah might be. Let me give you a call back in a little while, okay?"

Missy hung up and looked over at Echo.

"I have a feeling that today is going to be a long day," she sighed.

"Can we at least have cupcakes before we dive in?"

"Absolutely," Missy chuckled, heading for the display cases.

***

Missy stopped at the coffee shop where Grayson's fiancée Sarah used to work when she lived with her parents in Calgon. Poor Sarah had endured more tragedy in her young life than anyone should ever have to. Her mother had been psychotically controlling, never allowing Sarah to have friends or wear fashionable clothing, or even participate in school activities that she deemed inappropriate. The bitter woman had emotionally—and on occasion—physically abused her husband and daughter until one fateful day, Sarah's father snapped, killing her mother and burning the family home down in an attempt to hide the evidence.

He'd been in prison ever since, and when Grayson came down to visit Missy and Chas last Thanksgiving, Sarah had chosen to make a brand new start and gone to Louisiana with the shy young man when he returned. He'd offered her a job in the cupcake shop that Missy had given him when she left LaChance, and the two had fallen in love. Now the sweet young woman was missing, and Missy thought that she might just know where she'd disappeared to.

"Hi, may I help you?" the friendly young man behind the counter at the Mean Bean coffee shop asked.

Missy ordered a caramel latte, and while he prepared it, she peered around the espresso machine to talk with him.

"Have you worked here long?" she asked, watching him expertly froth the milk.

"Couple of years," he replied pleasantly.

"Did you know Sarah? She worked here last year around this time."

"Of course, yeah. She was really nice, we were sad to see her go, but I totally understood after what happened."

"Yeah, poor thing. Have you seen her lately?"

"I haven't, but my co-worker Ashley said that she came in a couple of days ago. Is she a friend of yours?"

"Oh yes, and she's marrying a very dear friend of mine," Missy smiled, relieved. Her hunch had been correct.

"Nice! Tell her congrats from Jeremy," the young man handed her the latte.

"I definitely will. Have a good day Jeremy."

"You too, ma'am, thanks."

***

It was a short ride from the Mean Bean to the empty lot where Sarah's family home once stood. Because her father had gone to prison, the home had never been rebuilt, and as Missy got out of the car, she saw the forlorn figure of Sarah sitting on what remained of the steps. Stepping delicately across the weed-choked former lawn, Missy made her way over to the young woman. Sarah's hair was haphazardly tossed into a messy bun, she wore no makeup, her clothing was dark and rumpled, and the poor thing looked terribly thin and pale. When she raised her head from her knees, seeing

Missy, tears ran down her face and she didn't bother wiping them away.

"Oh honey," Missy went to her, arms outstretched and embraced the waif, who began sobbing and apologizing.

"I'm sorry, I didn't mean to scare everyone… I just didn't know what to do, and I felt so bad and worthless… and couldn't figure out how someone as awesome as Grayson would want to marry a motherless misfit like me, whose dad is rotting away in prison," she cried, her frail shoulders shaking.

"Shhhh… it's going to be alright," Missy whispered, holding the miserable young woman tight and stroking her hair. When her sobs subsided a bit, several minutes later, Missy placed both her hands on Sarah's shoulders to make certain that she had her full attention.

"Now you listen to me, young lady," she said with a sad smile, her eyes moist. "You don't need to apologize. Most young brides get cold feet and they don't have nearly as good a reason as you do, okay?"

Sarah nodded, her lower lip trembling.

"And let me tell you something else, darlin… as long as I am on this earth drawing breath, you will never be motherless, do you understand me?"

Missy's own tears started flowing, which opened up Sarah's floodgates once again, so back into Missy's arms she went, crying until it was all out of her system, while Missy dug into her purse, pulling out tissue after tissue.

The two women sat side by side on the remains of the front steps, wiping eyes and noses, content for the moment just to be in each other's company. Missy took Sarah's hand and squeezed it.

"I want you to know that I love you, and Grayson loves you, and in just a few days, you're going to become that fine young man's wife. You two are a part of my family, and you're both going to make me so proud," she wrapped an arm around Sarah's shoulders, and the young woman leaned into her gratefully.

"I'm sorry that I scared Grayson," she murmured.

"Well, I'm taking you back to the inn with me. We'll get you set up in our guest room and you can take a nice hot bath and give that man of yours a call. He's been worried sick at the thought of losing you."

"I can't wait to hear his voice," Sarah admitted shyly. "I've missed him so much."

"Then let's get you home. We have a wedding to finish planning," Missy smiled and stood, offering her hand to Sarah, who clasped it as though she were hanging on for dear life.

"Yeah, let's go home," she nodded.

CHAPTER 8

Chas Beckett regarded the woman in his office. Petaluma Myers sat defiantly, arms crossed, legs splayed out in front of her, in the chair across from his desk.

"I don't have no idea what you're talking about, and I really want you to hurry up and get this over with so I can go have a cigarette," she complained, eyeing Chas with hostility.

"Ms. Myers, if you don't cooperate with my investigation by answering some questions, you may not be going anywhere other than a holding cell," the detective replied mildly. "We're here as a courtesy to you. If you're going to make this difficult, we can certainly relocate to an interrogation room."

"Well you don't have to get huffy about it," Petaluma pouted. "It ain't like I done somethin' wrong."

"Where were you between the hours of one and four o'clock this morning?" the detective ignored the commentary.

"How graphic do you want the details," she leered, giving him a lewd wink.

"Where were you?" Chas repeated, devoid of expression and wishing he had a strong cup of coffee and an air freshener.

"I was in bed with my man and we were…" she began playfully.

"Address?" the detective interrupted.

Petaluma gave him Steve's address.

"Tell me about your altercation with Nari Lee."

"My what, with who?" she blinked at him, befuddled.

"You had a disagreement with the young woman who worked at the flower shop," Chas prompted, trying not to sigh.

"Oh, pshhh… that wasn't nothing. She just thought that I was a sloppy old drunk, so I put her in her place. No biggie," she shrugged.

The detective stared at her for a moment. "Let's start at the beginning…"

***

After Missy had gotten Sarah settled into the guest room of the owner's quarters in the inn, her doorbell rang, and she closed her eyes briefly before going to answer it, hoping that nothing else catastrophic had happened.

Echo brushed past Missy when she opened the door and sat down on one of the barstools in the kitchen.

"You are not going to believe this," the wide-eyed redhead began.

"At this point, I'd believe just about anything," Missy sighed, putting water in the tea kettle and placing it on the stove. "What now?" she asked, not certain that she wanted to know.

"Kel and the realtor were doing another walk-through at my house, and when they came back out, they saw Petaluma being loaded into the back of a patrol car."

Missy blinked at her friend for a moment, at a loss, then plopped onto a barstool, dropping her head into her hands.

"Let me guess… drunk and disorderly?"

Echo shrugged her shoulders. "No idea."

"Did they take Steve too?"

"Nope, just her."

"Wow, I wonder if they had a fight and she hit him or something?" Missy mused, getting back up as the tea kettle started a low whistle.

"They didn't. Kel said that Petaluma was yelling and clinging to Steve until they held up handcuffs. Then she went quietly."

"Did he hear what they were saying?"

"No, but it was pretty clear that she wasn't happy about whatever it was."

"Great. Grayson's getting married in a few days and his mother may be in jail."

Neither woman had seen Sarah slip quietly into the room, and they were startled when she spoke.

"Petaluma is in jail?" she whispered, horrified.

"We don't know that for certain, honey," Missy held up a hand of caution. "But she did get into a patrol car."

"Why? What happened?"

"We don't know yet."

"I had no idea that she was even here. Grayson wasn't sure that she'd bother coming to the wedding."

"She's been here for a little while, staying with my next door neighbor," Echo explained. "It's a long story, but as soon as we find out what's happening, we'll let you know."

"Should I tell Grayson?" she asked, biting her lip.

"Let's just see what happens first," Missy advised. "There's no sense in upsetting him if we don't have to."

***

Before he had taken his wife out of town, Jeong Lee had gone to the floral shop where his stepdaughter worked. The concerned stepfather had come into Nari's room while Chas and his team were looking for clues, and turned over a videotape which clearly showed Petaluma yelling at and trying to intimidate his stepdaughter. The only alibi that Grayson's mother had was Loud Steve, who had allegedly been drinking with her and engaging in other various sorts of debauchery during the time period when Nari was murdered. While the evidence in the case so far was circumstantial, it certainly didn't paint a positive picture for Grayson's mother, whose status was moving from being a person of interest in the case to being a suspect.

Since the detective still wanted to do some digging into Nari's relationship with Logan Greitzer, he released Petaluma to Steve's care, with a stern warning that if she tried to leave town, she'd be arrested for murder. Chas had looked into the background of the councilman's son and had found some things that made him want to take a closer look. Some of the accusations that had been levelled at the entitled young man were apparently harmless, but when scrutinized together with other offenses and the fact that he'd been dating a murder victim, a more sinister picture began to emerge.

***

"Please note that there is indication of sexual activity. Samples were taken for possible DNA, and abrasions on the victim indicate that the encounter may not have been consensual. Also note that the victim was approximately nine weeks pregnant," Tim dictated to Fiona, as he examined the remains of Nari Lee.

"Holy cow, did the perp violate her before she was murdered?" his assistant asked.

"It's possible," he replied absently, intent upon his work.

"There is significant bruising on the back of the head."

"Blunt instrument?" Fiona asked, taking notes.

"Not likely. The indication is impact, as though the killer may have slammed her head against a wall, or the floor."

"Wow, sounds like there should be plenty of physical evidence left in the place where she was actually killed."

"One would presume," Tim murmured. "The lobes of the ears are torn, and the tearing took place post-mortem."

"Hmm… do you think that maybe her attacker was a thief, and they stole her earrings after they killed her?"

"I think that's perhaps what the perpetrator would like us to believe," the mortician blinked rapidly behind his thick glasses.

"You mean they did it as an afterthought to try to throw the police off?" Fiona raised an eyebrow.

"It's plausible," her boss nodded.

"But why would someone do that?"

"Usually to cover up the fact that the victim knew them. They throw in possibilities like rape and robbery to make it seem like the random, heinous act of a stranger."

"Makes sense. You're really good at this stuff, maybe you should have been a detective," she teased, knowing that Tim would be appalled at the suggestion.

"Nonsense, I've found my niche, thank you very much. Besides, why would I want to work with the living?" He continued his examination unperturbed.

***

"Felicia Derry?" Chas asked the young woman who answered the door of an expensive downtown apartment.

"Who wants to know?" she asked seductively, her eyes roving over the handsome detective.

"Detective Chas Beckett," was the reply as he flashed his badge.

The woman's demeanor changed instantly.

"I'm Felicia, what do you want?" she asked, wrapping her arms around her midsection.

"I need to ask you some questions, may I come in?"

"I have to get to work in like an hour and I still haven't had coffee, and…" she began backing away from the door, making excuses.

"I'm here as part of a homicide investigation. We can either talk here or I can take you down to the station and we can talk there, it's up to you," Chas' gaze was steely.

Felicia stopped short and stared at him with her elegant mouth open. "Homicide? Who was killed?" her eyes darted back and forth.

"Does that mean we're talking here?" the detective asked pointedly.

"Oh! Uh… yeah, come in. Don't mind the mess, the housekeeper doesn't come until tomorrow," she murmured, leading him into a tastefully decorated living room.

A Siamese cat meowed plaintively at them when they sat down, Felicia on the couch, Chas in a wing-back chair. When Felicia ignored the pampered pet, she began twining around Chas's ankles and purring, leaving a trail of silky fur on the bottom of his trouser legs. The detective couldn't help himself and reached down to pet the purring feline.

"She's friendly," he remarked, gazing into the cat's china-blue eyes.

"She hates men usually."

"At least she's a good judge of character," the detective quipped, then sat back up and took out his pen and notebook.

"So who died?" Felicia asked again.

"We'll get to that. I wanted to ask you about the nature of your relationship with Logan Greitzer."

"Logan? Why?" she seemed confused.

Chas merely raised an eyebrow, waiting for her to answer the question. She finally took the hint.

"I wouldn't call what I had with Logan a relationship," she replied at last, her tone tinged with what sounded like bitterness.

"What would you call it?" he asked, as the cat jumped lightly into his lap and lay down, purring. He'd have to use the lint roller that he kept in his glove compartment, but he didn't mind the presence of the lovely animal at all. Missy's dogs, a golden retriever named Toffee, and a maltipoo named Bitsy would subject him to some very suspicious sniffing when he got home.

"A sick and twisted arrangement if you must know," Felicia's voice was low.

"How so?"

"Logan and I had a wild night together last summer. We met at a party and continued the party afterwards on our own. When the police found us, we were naked at the beach and had some weed in our possession. Logan said his dad could get us out of trouble, but that I had to pay a price for it," she dropped her eyes as the color rose in her cheeks.

"What kind of price?"

"Sexual favors. I had to accommodate Logan whenever he came around, and he liked to play rough, if you know what I mean, so I finally told him I felt like I had 'paid' enough. He was angry and used me for a punching bag, but what he didn't know is that I had been worried about what he would do when I finally told him no, and I had set up cameras, which captured the whole interaction."

"Did you go to the police?" Chas asked, frowning. He didn't recall seeing any domestic violence reports under her name when he checked her records.

Felicia shook her head. "No. I used the same tactic that Logan did. I told him that I had the evidence, and that if he ever darkened my doorstep again, I'd use it. I also told him that if anything happened to me, my sister would go to the police with her copy of the tape."

"Did he know your sister?"

She barked a harsh, dry, humorless laugh. "Detective, I don't have a sister. Logan didn't even know me well enough to know that I was lying about that. He wasn't exactly big on conversation."

"I noticed," Chas commented dryly. "Has he bothered you since then?"

"He texted me once and I told him where he could go and how to get there."

"So, why are you telling me this now, if you didn't want to go to the police before?"

"Because I figure that if you're here asking about a homicide and the first name you mention is Logan Greitzer, either he upset the wrong person and got killed, or he killed someone and this stupid assault tape will be the least of his worries," she shrugged. "Besides, if he's either dead or going to jail, I don't have to watch my back anymore."

"Do you have the tape?" Chas asked.

"I have several. I made lots of copies, because, even though I don't have a sister, I do have friends who look out for me, and they have copies. They don't know what's on the tape, but they have copies."

"Do any of your friends know about Logan?"

"No, I never mention him to anyone, he's a pig," Felicia's lower lip trembled slightly before she intentionally set her mouth in a hard line.

"Just for the record, what do you do for a living?"

"I work in a jewelry store."

Chas nodded and handed her his card.

"Thank you for your time. If you think of anything else that you can tell me about Logan, please give me a call."

"There's nothing else to tell. Thankfully, I hardly know the scumbag."

SUMMER PRESCOTT

CHAPTER 9

Spencer knew better than to open his eyes when he regained consciousness. The only way he'd be able to learn more about his immediate environment would be to convince his foes that he was still unconscious. He made certain to keep his breathing at a slow, even pace, as though he was sleeping, and didn't allow his eyelids to even flicker. He couldn't swallow, that was a dead giveaway, so he simply allowed the saliva that pooled in his mouth to slide down the back of his throat on its own, thankful that he at least had been left lying on his back.

Listening to the breathing in the room, he detected at least four other people, and hoped that two of them might be Janssen and Steve Arnold. He did wonder if the foreign operatives had been sent in to rescue Steve, in which case, he and Janssen would be outnumbered. Looking through slitted lids, he noticed that the room in which he was being kept was not well lit. He tried to identify his location by any particular smells, and could only detect the scent of hamburgers hanging in the air. They had to have been recently consumed, and apparently someone in the room had been fond of raw onion.

Surely the operatives wouldn't have selected the kitchen as the best place for confining two of the most skilled men of "Command." Spencer and Janssen were known for being masters of escape, and had finessed their way out of captivity on too many occasions to count. Many times they had allowed themselves to be "captured" so that they could gain access to inner sanctums which would otherwise be closed to them. The two seasoned Marines were a formidable force, and Spencer was confident that it would only be a matter of time before they subdued the foreign operatives so that they could decide what needed to be done with Steve Arnold.

An ampule, designed to wake him up, was cracked open under his nostrils, and he pretended to regain consciousness, making note of all that he saw, immediately upon opening his eyes.

He didn't recognize the swarthy man standing over him with an automatic weapon.

"Wake up," the operative ordered, kicking Spencer in the ribs.

The Marine had been secured to a portable cot, with rope and duct tape. There were bonds and strips of tape across his legs, arms, torso and neck, and though he felt like he had some freedom of motion, he didn't move, not wanting the foreign operatives to know that he wasn't as tightly bound as they thought. He wasn't being kept in the kitchen either, though there was a plate with a half-eaten burger near his head that was probably placed there to confuse his senses and arouse his hunger. They were in one of the bunk rooms of the confinement facility, rather than in a cell, which Spencer found strange until he realized that the cells had windows, where outsiders could see whether or not there were lights or shadows moving about inside, whereas the bunk rooms had concrete walls with no windows, a perfect place to hunker down and wait for your prey to come to you.

Steve Arnold had blood on his shirt, but didn't appear to be wounded. He was also secured to a cot and was giving Spencer what looked like an apologetic look, something that was quite unusual for him. It took a tremendous amount of strength for the Marine not to react when he saw Janssen strapped to a cot like he was. His friend's color was grey, and he was sweating profusely. His eyes were glazed and staring off into an uninhabited corner of the room, and now that Spencer was more in tune with sensory information, he could smell the infection that oozed from bullet wounds that Janssen had sustained. It did not look good for the scarred Marine, and Spencer's blood boiled. He had to get his friend some medical attention immediately. Janssen was not going to leave this world suffering on a cot in the middle of nowhere. No way. When his friend passed into the hereafter, it would most certainly be as the result of a valiant warrior's death.

The phone in the hand of the other foreign operative rang, and he answered in Farsi. Clearly he had no idea that Spencer, Janssen, and Arnold knew the language well enough to speak and understand it, so he stayed in the room to have a conversation with someone who was apparently a high ranking official.

"Yes sir, we have three of them. The target and two operatives. Yes sir, I am aware of that, but the target was accompanied by one operative and another came later. No sir, we do not have the information yet. Yes, I'm well aware of who they work for. No I don't want the wrath of the U.S. government and Beckett Holdings to fall upon our heads. Should I just kill the target then? What would you have me do? I see. I heartily disagree, sir. Yes sir, I understand."

With a muttered curse, the second man hung up the phone and turned to the first. Still speaking in Farsi, the two men conversed, entirely unaware that Steve and Spencer were listening intently. To his credit, Steve managed to not react when the operative asked for permission to kill him.

"That was the Director."

"I figured that. What did he want?"

"He said that we jeopardized the entire mission by taking the operatives. We were only supposed to take the target. The U.S. government could see the target as being expendable, but the others are too valuable to Beckett Holdings. Repercussions for killing them would be profound."

"So, if we can't kill them, what are we supposed to do with them?"

"The Director said to release them," the foreign operative made a disgusted face.

"After putting our lives in danger to secure them? Ridiculous."

"You and I agree. The Director does not. If he says let them go, we let them go."

"What if we don't?"

"What do you mean?"

"He said we have to leave them alone, right? So let's leave them alone," he gestured to the three bound men.

His partner finally caught on.

"You mean leave them like this and walk away?"

"Exactly. Leave them to try and escape, but don't help them to do so. If they die, they die because of their lack of strength and skills, not because we killed them. Our conscience is clear."

"But what happens when the Americans come in and find them dead?"

"It doesn't matter. We'll be long gone and they'll have no idea who to blame."

The other man's face broke into a grin and he nodded, sadistically pleased.

"It's settled then, we'll *leave them alone*."

The man nearest Spencer gave him a hard kick and followed the other man out of the room. There were a few noises as the men prepared to leave, then the clanging of the heavy metal security door, and finally silence.

"You'd better find a way to get freed up fast, Janssen doesn't have much time left," Steve rasped from across the room.

Spencer knew what he had to do and it would take a tremendous amount of strength to do it. He cleared his mind, focusing on his muscles, which he relaxed. Taking deep breaths, he prepared himself for what would undoubtedly be a difficult and painful experience. Janssen's life hung in the balance and the Marine would do whatever he had to in order to save him. A few more deep breaths and he was ready.

He drew in one last big breath, and lightning fast, he tensed every muscle in his upper body, thrusting his shoulders, chest, and midsection toward a sitting-up position. The cot that he was strapped to creaked and groaned, but only budged a bit, so he rested for a moment, then tried again, his abs, back, shoulder, and neck muscles bulging with the effort. The creaking of the wooden frame was a bit louder this time, but his muscles gave way before the cot did.

Spencer deliberately relaxed his muscles, panting with exertion. Sweat had soaked through his shirt and ran from his forehead in rivulets. His powerful muscles twitched and burned but he had to try again. He feared he only had the strength for one more attempt, so the third time had to be the charm, or they'd all die. The Marine closed his eyes, getting in touch with every individual fiber of his being, and steadied his breath, preparing.

He lurched forward one last time and heard the satisfying crack of one side of the cot snapping in half. The action caused the entire cot to flip onto its side, but it freed Spencer's left hand without crushing it in the process. Wiggling the hand out of the rope and tape, he worked his arm out and untied the knots of rope on the left side of the cot, no easy task while lying on his left side. Once the rope had been untied, he tore through the duct tape as if it were tissue paper, adrenaline giving him preternatural strength. Once freed, he grabbed a knife out of the stash that the foreign operatives had left on the table to taunt them, and cut Steve's hands free so that he could free himself while Spencer went to work on Janssen's bonds.

"Don't worry Marine, we'll get you out of this," he muttered, slicing through rope and tape carefully but quickly.

The heat rolled off Janssen in waves, and dark lines of infection had started to appear on his arms and legs. Spencer knew that timing was crucial, if he didn't attack the infection immediately, Janssen could be dead within hours. Once his buddy had been freed, he ordered Steve, who was still working on his bonds, to stay put, and sprinted for the medical supply room. The confinement facility was equipped with a decent supply of antibiotics, and Spencer grabbed an IV bag, syringes and lines so that he could inject Janssen immediately, then get him set up with a steady infusion of medicine. All "Command" operatives were trained as combat medics, needing to know enough to be able to keep themselves and fellow operatives alive under most circumstances. The unfortunate thing was that these were not "most circumstances," and the next hours would determine whether the scarred Marine on the cot lived or died.

Once Spencer had the initial dose given, and the IV in place, he had to go to work on finding and cleaning Janssen's wounds. Steve had finally removed all of his tape and rope and stood behind Spencer, watching as he efficiently took care of the wounded Marine.

"I'll go get hot water and towels," he said quietly, disappearing.

Spencer had his doubts as to whether he'd ever see Steve again, figuring he'd escape while Spencer was preoccupied with saving Janssen's life, but he came jogging back a few minutes later, a first aid kit and towels under his arms, carrying a huge tub of water, a container of salt hanging from his mouth. Spencer nodded his thanks, then used a huge hunting knife to cut away Janssen's clothing so that he could see what he was dealing with.

The Marine had been hit twice in his left leg and once in his left arm. Every bullet hole oozed with foul-smelling pus, and Steve peered over Spencer's shoulder, concerned.

"If they used "dirty" bullets, you could be putting your own safety at risk."

"I'll take my chances," Spencer muttered.

"At least put some gloves on. You know the protocol," Steve said gravely, handing him a pair of nitrile gloves, which Spencer snapped on quickly.

"Protocol would suggest that I kill you where you stand, but I don't have the luxury of time at the moment," the Marine rumbled, turning his full attention to swabbing out the oozing wounds with gauze and salt water, while Janssen, too weak even to writhe, merely grimaced in pain.

"Dump some of that clean water over here to rinse this wound, while I work on the leg," he commanded, and Steve rushed to do his bidding.

When he'd rinsed the wound, he patted it dry with one of the towels.

"Put topical antibiotics on there and cover it with a bandage," Spencer barked out orders while he scraped and wiped infection from Janssen's leg. "He's lucky that the bullets passed all the way through. At least they're not in there festering."

Steve pulled on a pair of gloves and went to work on the arm wound. The two unlikely medics had just finished covering the leg wounds with gauze when Janssen let out a weak, but agonized moan.

"Go grab me two doses of morphine," Spencer's jaw tightened and he took his gloves off, placing a hand on Janssen's forehead. The antibiotics hadn't knocked back the fever yet, the Marine was still burning up.

Steve came sprinting back to the room with the morphine and Spencer hooked the time-release bag up to the IV drip, hoping to bring at least some relief to his buddy. If Janssen could sleep through the worst of it, his body would have time to rest, heal, and let the antibiotics do their job. The two men carefully pulled the sodden and reeking blankets out from under his body, covering him with fresh linen. He was now as clean, dry and warm as they could get him without traumatizing him further by moving him. Spencer would stand watch over his friend for as long as it took to get a helicopter to the facility and airlift Janssen out. They would then head to the airport where a jet would be waiting, with medical staff aboard, to transport them to the private medical facility on the Beckett estate in upstate New York. With one short text, help was on the way, and the Marine stationed himself by Janssen's side, pulling a chair over to keep watch.

Steve Arnold stood on the opposite side of Janssen's cot, regarding Spencer gravely.

"Those bullets were meant for me," he said quietly.

"Figured," Spencer refused to look at him.

"He saved my life. I wouldn't have survived this. He literally pushed me out of the line of fire and took the hits. He brought me out here to threaten me, maybe kill me, and he ended up saving my life," Steve shook his head.

"He wouldn't have killed you. It's not who he is. Only way he would've killed you is if you had tried to kill him. Who were those men?"

"They were a part of the coup that you and Janssen helped shut down years ago. They've got a guy on the inside at Beckett Holdings, and they wanted to take me out so they could learn the identities of "Command" operatives and Beckett agents. Once I talked, they'd dispose of me."

"Did you?"

"Talk? Heck no. I'd die first."

"Then why didn't they kill you?"

"My guess is that they didn't have the authority. They obviously didn't know who you and Janssen were, but whoever they talked to on the phone did. Someone higher up made the decision to keep me alive. Probably because Janssen was here and it could've caused an international incident if something happened to him... or you."

"So you're on the run now?"

"No. I'm done."

"Done?"

"Done. You two saved my life. I'm not going to track you for Command anymore. I'm going to make arrangements for them to finally release you, once and for all. They can ask for your help in the future, but there won't be any more strong-arm tactics. You and Janssen can have your real names back, become members of society again. I'm done," Steve hung his head, the weight of his misdeeds on behalf of his country weighing heavily on his shoulders.

"I'll believe it when I see it," Spencer muttered, staring down at Janssen, watching for any sign of change.

"You won't have to take my word for it. I'll accompany you to the Beckett estate and wait there until the Big Man arrives with your walking papers."

"You're serious?" the Marine finally glanced at the man who had been hounding his every footstep for as long as he could remember.

"Dead serious."

The full implication of Steve's words slammed into Spencer like a ton of bricks. If what he said was true, he and Janssen would never have to hide from the government again. They'd be... free. Men who could walk around with a clear conscience in the land of the free, home of the brave. It sounded way too good to be true.

CHAPTER 10

"We sprayed the victim's bedroom down with Luminol and it lit up like a Christmas tree," the forensics tech reported. "The patterns indicate that she was brutally attacked in her room, bled most of the way out, and was moved afterwards. The mattress was flipped, and the underside was bloody, but the sheets and blankets were clean. Pillowcases too. We've got guys doing a sweep in the area around where she was found, to attempt to locate the linens, the killer's clothing, and the murder weapon."

Chas nodded. "Thanks for the report. The coroner said that we're looking for a large kitchen knife, and the Lees reported that they were missing one. Black handle, three screws."

"Gotcha. Oh, and we found some hairs that didn't belong to anyone in the family. They were on the clean pillowcase."

"Any guesses as to where they came from?" the detective sat forward.

"Nah, it's weird. Because of the violence, I had just assumed that our perp was a guy, but either our dude has really long hair, or the perp is a female," the tech shrugged.

Chas Beckett sat back in his chair, tenting his fingers under his chin. It seemed that Petaluma wasn't quite in the clear yet, despite some very incriminating information about Logan Greitzer. Sighing, he knew that he'd have to interview Grayson's mother again today, but first he wanted to have lunch with his wife, so he said goodbye to the tech, grabbed his keys and headed for home.

***

"Honey, you don't actually think that Petaluma Myers killed that poor sweet girl, do you?" Missy asked, as she and Chas enjoyed the fresh air and seafood at their favorite beachside restaurant.

They hadn't had much time together lately with their busy schedules, so they had made a date to meet today for a nice lunch.

"I honestly don't know what to think," her handsome husband admitted, running a frustrated hand through his hair.

"You'll figure it out," Missy kissed his stubbly cheek. The poor man had been so busy that he'd run out without shaving this morning. "What about that awful son of a councilman?"

"I'm still looking at him too, but you're not supposed to know that," he smiled indulgently.

"My lips are sealed, darlin," she promised. "Is there anything I can do to help?"

Chas kissed his wife's forehead, loving her sweetness and kind heart.

"Absolutely. You can focus entirely on getting ready for Grayson's wedding and let me handle the police work," he teased.

"But, I…" she began, but he touched a fingertip to her lips, shushing her.

"I can work on finding out if Petaluma is innocent if I don't have to worry about you going out and doing dangerous things."

"Fine," Missy sighed. "You taste like ketchup by the way," she grinned.

"You're welcome," he chuckled, gathering their plates to take up to the service window.

***

"I done told you, I ain't got nothin' to do with that girl dyin,'" Petaluma stood her ground, hands on hips when Chas came to Loud Steve's house to interview her again.

Today she was clad in shiny blue stretchy capris and a star-spangled tube top slipping lower by the second. She took her hands off her hips for a moment to hitch up her top in a huff.

"If you have nothing to do with it, then you shouldn't have a problem with me taking a look around, right?" he asked reasonably.

"This ain't even my house, I'm just staying here. This is Stevie's place," she shrugged, making the tube top dance lower, much to the detective's chagrin.

"Well, I happen to know that 'Stevie' has several unpaid traffic fines that we could issue a warrant on if it came to that," Chas was unblinking.

"Oh, now that ain't nice," she sighed. "Fine, if you're gonna be a poop about it, come on in and have your look, but don't expect me to babysit you. I'm going outside to have a cigarette."

"I think that'd be best," he replied dryly.

Chas started out by doing a quick sweep through all the rooms of the house, wondering how in the world people managed to survive in such squalor, and stopped short beside a long and low dresser in Steve's bedroom. Something sparkly caught his eye, and he bent down, shining his flashlight between the back of the dresser and the wall. Taking his pen, he used the end of it to coax out a necklace that looked very expensive. It was a simple platinum and diamond pendant, in the shape of the letter N. Pulling a photo of Nari Lee out of his blazer pocket, he looked closely and saw the lovely necklace around her neck.

The detective pulled out his phone and called in forensics to do a thorough investigation of Steve's house. After calling in the team, he went outside to find Petaluma, as promised, smoking a cigarette on the back patio.

"See, told you that you weren't gonna find nothin," she rolled her eyes, blowing out a puff of smoke.

"Right," Chas said agreeably. "My team will be here in a few minutes just to make sure though."

"Well shoot, how many folks you gonna have traipsin' through here today, geez…" she complained.

She continued to grumble about paying taxes and getting harassed and various other nonsensical things, but she'd lost the detective's attention. His gaze was focused on what looked like a freshly dug up patch of earth under a shrub by the corner of the patio. Making a mental note to check the spot out when the forensics team arrived, he pretended to listen to Petaluma's grousing, thinking through the things he'd found thus far.

"Petaluma, baby, is this dude botherin' you?" Steve came out the back door and saw Chas sitting with his girl.

"Nah, he's just lookin' for evidence and stuff," she waved breezily. "Come give your mama some sugar," she batted her eyes in a manner that looked ludicrous on a late forty-something.

"I don't know if I like you lookin' through my stuff. I got rights, ya know," Steve postured.

Chas raised an eyebrow.

"So, Stevie, the detective said you had some unpaid traffic fines or somethin… ?"

The unkempt man paused, frowning. "Well, yeah, but there ain't no warrant out on me," he said uncertainly.

"There could be," Chas stared him down.

"Well… fine. Look around and do what you need to do, but make it quick," he groused.

"We'll take as much time as we need. That'll be all right with you, won't it?" It wasn't a question.

"Fine, whatever," Steve replied, sinking into a plastic molded chair that flexed under his bulk.

Chas tapped out a text to the lead tech, who was on his way to the house.

"When you arrive, send a tech to the back patio. I think there may be something buried back here."

The detective made a pretense of needing to take a look at the front yard, so that Steve and Petaluma would follow him, and less than two minutes later, the tech who had gone to the back patio texted Chas that he had a knife that fit the description of the murder weapon. It had been unearthed from beneath the bush where the detective had noticed the loose soil.

"Would you come with me for just a moment?" Chas calmly led Petaluma into the house where a handful of forensics techs and a couple of uniformed officers were moving deliberately through the house, searching for more evidence. Taking her to the uniformed duo, Chas turned her over, telling them to put her, and Steve in holding cells to await questioning. They'd just become primary suspects. The detective would question them, and try to find out more about Logan Greitzer. Both of them had the odds stacked against them, it was now just a matter of figuring out who actually had killed Nari Lee.

Chas left the scene a short time later and went back to the station, where his already long and eventful day got a little bit longer. When he passed by an interrogation room, he saw Logan Greitzer sitting sullenly in an uncomfortable plastic chair, a paper cup of water in front of him. There was a uniformed officer outside the door, making a note on an official form.

"What's the story?" Chas asked, inclining his head toward Logan.

"We got an anonymous tip that a bartender from the Seaport Lounge saw Logan at closing time on the night that Nari Lee was killed, so we checked out the area around the Seaport and found a bunch of bloody linens in their dumpster. The lab guys are testing now to see if there's a match with the victim. We went looking for Greitzer an his mom said that he wasn't home, so we went by the Lee house on a hunch and found him trying to break into the victim's room."

Chas frowned. Nothing was adding up. Just when the evidence seemed to point to Logan, there were discoveries made at Petaluma's. After new evidence incriminating her appeared, Logan resurfaced again, looking guilty. Could they have been working together? It was time to find out. He stepped into the room with the angry young man, who didn't even bother to acknowledge his presence.

"We meet again," the detective remarked, sitting across the interrogation table from Logan.

No response, not even the briefest eye contact.

"You're not doing yourself any favors by not cooperating, you know."

Logan glanced up briefly, glared at Chas and resumed staring at the wall.

"There was some very interesting evidence that was found this evening. I'd say we found it right about the time you were caught trying to break into your ex-girlfriend's house. You know, one of the worst mistakes a criminal can make is in thinking that there were no witnesses to see whatever they may have done. Then a witness comes out of the woodwork and boom, a conviction. A lot of guys go down like that, Logan."

"So," he finally muttered, defiant.

"So, if you don't start talking, maybe the witness who saw you out at a bar on the night that Nari was killed, instead of at home in bed like you said, will start talking instead. I hear he has a lot to say. You lied, Logan… why?"

"You have no idea what you're talking about, Mr. Civil Servant," the young man rolled his eyes and went back to his vow of silence.

Chas was a bit thrown off. He'd expected the kid to crack like an aged walnut, but he hadn't even flinched. That kind of sociopathic confidence was rare at his age, unless he was a serial killer or something, a possibility that the detective didn't even want to consider at the moment.

"Detective Beckett?" a uniformed cop opened the door after rapping on it lightly.

"Yeah, what's up?" Chas asked, mildly irritated at the interruption.

"Councilman Greitzer is here to see you… with his attorney."

"Of course he is," the detective sighed, running a hand through his hair. "Send him in."

The councilman breezed in, supremely confident, briefly shooting his son a warning look, and shook Chas' hand. The two had met before, at charity events, but didn't know each other well. Councilman Greitzer introduced his attorney, Marty Nussbaum, with whom the detective was also familiar. Marty was known for being the defender of the rich and shameless, and he rarely lost his cases.

The two well-dressed men sat like expensive bookends on either side of Logan Greitzer, facing Chas. Marty had a briefcase with him that he oddly hadn't opened yet.

"My client is willing to pay a fine for accidentally trespassing on private property earlier this evening, with the understanding that you will drop any further investigation regarding his potential involvement in the Nari Lee case," the attorney began, without preamble.

"Rather interesting that you're offering a deal, and a ridiculous one at that, without having even spoken to "your client," Chas observed. "And I'm not the DA, I don't make deals."

"It is my understanding that Mr. Greitzer is a person of interest in the murder of Nari Lee, is that correct?" Marty asked, ignoring the detective's comment entirely.

"Actually, with the tip and associated evidence that we received this evening, his status in the case will be reclassified to primary suspect."

"The anonymous tip, and the associated evidence were either fabricated or planted," the attorney announced.

"I'm supposed to believe that?" Chas raised his eyebrows.

"We have proof."

"Proof? What kind of proof?"

"Video proof, with time and date stamps. Do you have video proof from your anonymous report?" Marty challenged.

"We're working on getting in from the bar, so we don't have it yet, but we will."

"You might want to hold off on naming Mr. Greitzer as a primary suspect until you have that tape, because it will show you that my client was not at a bar on the night of the murder, and I have proof of exactly where he was during the hours in question," he patted the briefcase smugly.

"Fine, let's see it," Chas called his bluff.

"I'm afraid it's not that simple," the councilman broke in, receiving a scathing look from his attorney.

"What the councilman meant to say is that there are certain activities which take place on the videotape that would have to be overlooked in the interest of justice for my client," Marty covered smoothly.

"So, what you'd like me to believe is that you have a tape which proves that your client is innocent of the Lee murder, but which implicates him in another matter… is that what I'm hearing here?" Chas asked.

"There would need to be a blanket immunity from prosecution extended to my client before we could allow you to view the tape," the attorney clarified.

"There's no way that I can agree to that and you know it, There's also the matter of him trying to break into the Lee residence," the detective stared him down.

"Fine then. If you charge him, we'll see you in court. You'll have wasted your time pursuing the wrong suspect, and the actual killer will still be at large. Hope your conscience can live with that, Detective Beckett," Marty stood to go. "I'm assuming that you're not detaining my client for further questioning at this time?"

"No, get him out of here," Chas growled. "But if he leaves the state, I'll charge you with aiding a fugitive."

"I'm shaking in my boots," Marty smirked, while the councilman avoided the detective's eyes and hurried his son from the room.

Logan and his bookends passed Petaluma and Steve being led in while they were on the way out, and there didn't seem to be any flicker of recognition. All three of the men leaving merely overlooked the loud couple that was protesting their innocence nonstop. Chas yawned and stretched and headed for the coffee maker. He needed caffeine to get through the contradictory evidence in this bizarre case.

The detective had just sat down behind his desk when the buzzer on his office phone went off.

"Beckett," he answered, eyes closed, taking a sip of Mississippi mud that burned its way down his throat.

"There's a Mr. Lee here to see you," the desk sergeant reported.

"Send him over."

Jeong Lee appeared in the detective's doorway and Chas waved him in, indicating a chair across the desk.

"What can I do for you, Mr. Lee?

"We just got back into town and I heard that some suspects had been detained. Have you found the killer?" the worried stepfather asked.

"We're still looking into some things," Chas said. "Can I take your jacket? It's a bit warm in here," the detective smiled apologetically.

"Yes, thank you. There were police officers at my house when I arrived, but they wouldn't tell me much. Is there anything that I should know?"

"I think we're getting close. We're questioning a handful of suspects, and we've found more evidence…"

"Have you found the murder weapon?" Jeong interrupted.

"I'm sorry, I can't comment on exactly what evidence we have. It's way too early in the case, and if the press found out, we could lose our edge. I'm sure you understand."

"Oh yes, of course," he nodded. "I just want the monster who did this to our little girl to be brought to justice," he sighed, shaking his head.

"Well, that's what we want too," Chas assured him.

The two men chatted for a few more minutes, and Jeong remembered something.

"Oh, I nearly forgot, when we returned home, my wife found something underneath Nari's dresser when she was looking for her address book. It's probably nothing, but I thought you might want to look at it just in case," he reached into his pants pocket and brought out a small plastic bag which contained a tiny, pearl-handled pocket knife.

Chas took the bag, turning it back and forth to take a closer look at the pocket knife.

"Did your daughter carry a pocket knife?" he asked, still examining it through the bag.

"Oh definitely not, she was a glam girl," Jeong smiled sadly.

"Were any of her friends outdoorsy types?"

"No, not at all. That's why we brought this to you. It seemed so out of place that we thought it might be a clue."

"Good thinking," Chas nodded. "I'll check it out and see what we come up with."

"I really appreciate your thoroughness, Detective," Mr. Lee rose to go.

"Not a problem," he took Jeong's blazer down from the coat tree behind his desk and handed it to him. "I'll let you know if there are any breaks in the case."

"Thank you, Detective Beckett. Have a good night."

"You too," Chas showed him to the door, not looking forward to interviewing Petaluma and Loud Steve. He briefly considered going home and doing it in the morning, but since he was already here and had consumed at least half a cup of the station's strong, thick coffee, he figured that he might as well get it over with.

He dropped the pocket knife off in the lab to be dusted for fingerprints and swabbed for blood, then went to an interrogation room to wait for Petaluma to be brought up from the holding cell.

CHAPTER 11

Sarah, Missy, and Echo sat at their favorite table in the cupcake shop, discussing their plan for the day. It was time to finalize everything for the wedding, and all three women were stressed out because they were running out of time.

"Oh my goodness, these strawberry dream cupcakes are amazing," Sarah exclaimed, biting deeply into the small pink cakes that had just been frosted.

Of course there was a vegan version for Echo, and the pregnant mama had allowed herself the luxury of having two this morning, rationalizing that she'd be so active with shopping and planning that she'd work off the extra calories.

"Thanks, I had a craving for strawberry shortcake and modified a recipe to make cupcakes that tasted like it," Missy grinned, refilling Sarah's coffee cup and bringing Echo a fresh herbal tea bag. "So, here's a schedule I thought would be efficient for today," she said, handing over sheets of paper to Echo and Sarah.

Sarah nodded her approval, reading aloud.

"Cupcakes with Missy first, I like that. Then finding a cake topper and taking it to the cake artist, paying the deposit to the caterer, hitting the craft stores for table and reception hall decorations, paying the florist, and…"

"Hey," Echo interrupted. "Speaking of the florist—was Chas able to rule out Petaluma as a suspect?"

Missy shrugged. "I have no idea. He came home in the wee hours of the morning, slept for a couple of hours, then headed out again, so I didn't have a chance to talk to him."

"It couldn't possibly be Petaluma," Sarah said sadly. "Hopefully he's discovered that by now."

"Well, maybe if we get done with our errands early enough, we can stop by Loud Steve's and check on her. She'd probably be glad to see you," Missy smiled at Sarah.

"Oh, don't be so sure. The last time she came into the store back home, she yelled at me and accused me of trying to snatch her baby out from under her nose. She was drunk and wouldn't leave, so finally the man from the hardware store next door came over and helped Grayson get her out of there," the young woman blushed, remembering.

"Well, look at the bright side, we won't have to pay for entertainment at the reception," Echo snickered. Missy and Sarah just stared at her. "What? I thought it was funny," she muttered, taking a huge bite of cupcake.

The bell over the door jangled, and Izzy Gilmore walked in. Sarah's mouth dropped open in surprise as she recognized one of her favorite authors standing in front of her, live and in person.

"Hey Izzy! How've you been darlin? We haven't seen you in ages," Missy hugged the pale, thin young woman hard, and invited her to join them.

"Oh, life's been interesting," the author hedged, keeping the hand with the amputated finger in her lap. "I'm working on another book, so I've been holed up with that, but I wanted to see daylight, so I figured I'd be safe here," she said, kicking herself for revealing too much. Fortunately, no one picked up on her slip.

"Safe from the monsters you create in your books?" Echo teased.

"Something like that," Izzy gave a wan smile.

"You look a bit peaked," Missy noticed. "Can I get you some cupcakes and coffee?"

"Oh yes, please. And if you have something with caramel on it, that would really make my day."

"One coffee with caramel creamer and a vanilla caramel delight coming right up," she promised, heading behind the counter.

Echo introduced Sarah and Izzy while Missy was gone.

"So you're getting married in a few days? Wow, that's great! Congratulations," Izzy said, making Sarah's day.

The author hid the sadness and squashed the vision of Spencer that popped into her mind when she thought about love and commitment. She was determined to get over him, no matter what. When Missy set her coffee down in front of her, it was hard to get the warm, sweet liquid past the lump in her throat at first.

"So, the girls and I are running errands to take care of the last minute details for the wedding. Now, I know you're an introvert and all, but I'd love it if you'd join us. We're going to have a ball and I want you to come along," Missy said, putting Izzy on the spot.

"Well... I... it's Sarah's day..." she blushed.

"Oh, I'd love it if you came along too!" Sarah exclaimed excitedly. "How many brides get to run their wedding errands with their favorite author?" she giggled.

Izzy nodded, still blushing. "Well, okay then, if you really don't mind..."

"Of course she doesn't mind, silly," Echo teased. "It's settled then. Let's gobble up these cupcakes and hit the road, ladies, we've got a mission to complete."

***

"What do you mean Petaluma is in jail?" Missy demanded, when Chas finally came home.

"I'm sorry, sweetie, there are several things that seem to point to her involvement in Nari Lee's death, and until I can either prove or disprove them, she's going to stay put for a bit," the weary detective explained.

"But sugar, the wedding is just days away. You and I both know that she didn't do it, and we need to have her out of there by Friday for the rehearsal dinner."

"Missy, I know that you mean well, but it's just not that simple. I can't put a murder investigation on hold simply because it conflicts with a wedding," he sighed.

"I know," she bit her lip, worried. "I just haven't told Grayson about any of the murder stuff yet. I was hoping she'd be proved innocent long before it became an issue. I know you're doing your best, darlin."

"I'm trying, and I think I'm close, but I will have to go back into the office tonight."

"Can we take the girls for a walk first?"

"That sounds like a great idea," Chas agreed. There was nothing quite like a walk on the beach with Toffee, their sweet-tempered golden retriever, and Bitsy, the rambunctious maltipoo, to help him clear his head and lower his blood pressure.

His wife, the waves and the cool sand underfoot needed to work their magic so that he could get this case solved... for lots of reasons. Missy rose from the couch and smiled lovingly at her husband, offering her hand. He took it and they walked to the foyer to get the leashes.

***

"I've never seen so much pink in my life," Echo commented, wrapping the stem of a silk hydrangea in pink ribbon.

"It's my favorite color," Sarah shrugged. "I was never allowed to wear pink when I was growing up, so I want as much of it as I can get now."

Izzy stared at the bride-to-be as though she'd just declared that she was from outer space.

"What do you mean you weren't allowed to wear pink when you were growing up?" she asked, baffled.

Sarah and Echo exchanged a look.

"My mother was... different. She didn't let me wear pink because she said it was a frivolous color that would cause me to be paid undue attention and that I should be more modest," Sarah shrugged.

"That's awful," Izzy exclaimed, then clapped her hands over her mouth. "I'm sorry, I didn't mean to say that your mom..." she blushed to the roots of her hair.

"No, it's okay," Sarah smiled at her. "It was awful. I couldn't wear any of the pretty colors that I liked. No yellow, orange, red, purple... I hated it. When I got a job I used to hide normal clothes and change when I got to work."

"Normal clothes?" Izzy was fascinated.

"Yeah. My mom made all of my clothes. I always wore long skirts and long-sleeved shirts in greys and browns and dark blues. I didn't even know what jeans were until I started working."

"Wow. Well, you look great now."

"Thanks. I made it my policy to wear all of the colors that I couldn't wear when I was a kid, so you can usually see me coming a mile away," Sarah laughed self-consciously.

"Good for you," Izzy nodded her approval. "Let's make this the pinkest pink wedding that anyone has ever seen."

"Here's to pink power," Echo grinned.

"Izzy... you'll come to my wedding, won't you?" Sarah asked shyly.

"I'd be honored to. Should I wear a pink dress?"

"What else would you wear?" Sarah teased, and the two very different young women burst into laughter like old friends.

Echo had noticed something when Izzy covered her mouth moments before, and her curiosity got the best of her.

"Izzy, what happened to your finger?" she asked, when the laughter had died down.

The author self-consciously dropped her hand down into her lap. I had an accident involving a door and the door won. I lost the tip of my pinkie, so it has to stay wrapped up until I get my stitches out," she explained, avoiding their eyes.

"Oh, that's terrible," Sarah was wide-eyed.

"Yes, it was," Izzy agreed, thinking how horrified they'd be if they knew the truth.

"Is that going to affect your writing?" Echo wondered.

"I've already figured out how to compensate for it," the author shrugged. "My typing speed is only fractionally slower. It turns out that I hardly ever use my pinkies, so it wasn't too big of a deal. Hey, how many table toppers do we need to get done tonight?" she asked, changing the subject.

"As many as we can," Sarah replied. "Whatever we don't finish tonight, we can do tomorrow. That is if you're not sick of pink wedding stuff by then."

"Never. I live for pink wedding stuff," Izzy grinned, glad that her deflection had worked. "Maybe, if we have time after, we could go shopping for a dress for me to wear," she suggested, stepping firmly outside of her comfort zone.

"That would be fun," Sarah agreed enthusiastically.

Izzy figured that since it seemed that fate would never allow her to meet a man that she'd consider marrying, she might as well make the most of her new friend's wedding. She went home and took a long, tearful shower, slipping into bed afterward, feeling her heart break into tiny pieces all over again.

CHAPTER 12

The private jet had barely touched down on the Beckett estate's private air strip when Janssen went into convulsions. The hospital staff had an ambulance waiting on the tarmac, and they loaded the gravely ill Marine into it, speeding toward the state-of-the-art hospital facility housed in an underground complex on the vast estate. Spencer and Steve Arnold piled into an armor-plated black car with tinted windows and followed closely.

Spencer was stunned that, so far it looked as though Steve was going to live up to his promise to end the government's interest in the two Marines. He thought that the former watchdog would try to give him the slip at some point, but it seemed as though much of the fight had gone out of the once-powerful handler of operatives. For now, however, his attention was focused on Janssen as his scarred brother fought for his life.

When Spencer tried to follow Janssen's stretcher into the treatment room, he was detained by a wall of four operatives. He could have taken them out quickly and quietly and was preparing to do precisely that, when a hand on his shoulder and a familiar voice stopped him.

"Let them work, son," Chalmers, former manservant, now tasked with running an empire, had appeared just when the Marine needed him most. "Come on now, we have things to discuss," the elderly man coaxed, seeing the Marine's rapid blinking as his throat worked convulsively.

Steve Arnold tactfully looked away as the old man squeezed Spencer's shoulder and urged him toward the exit. He followed behind them a few paces, not knowing, nor wanting to know what words of comfort Chalmers might be offering to the strong, capable young man who had been like a member of the Beckett family for years.

The three men filed silently into Chalmers's study, and the geriatric, but still sharp, director of Beckett Holdings Corp. poured them each three fingers of scotch. No one said a word for several minutes as the men sipped and reined in thoughts and emotions in their own way.

"I've instructed the medical staff to contact me immediately if Janssen's condition changes," he told Spencer. "In the meantime, we need to discuss where we go from here," Chalmers folded his hands on the desk.

"Not to interrupt, but I may have some input into that," Steve Arnold offered, clearing his throat.

Chalmers regarded him with thinly veiled contempt. "Oh?" he raised an eyebrow skeptically.

"I'm Steve Arnold, I work with…"

"I know who you are. I knew who you were before you were ever aware of my existence, so don't waste our time with introductions. Say your piece and I'll decide what we're going to do with you," the dignified gentleman stated simply, his typically gentle eyes steely.

Steve blinked at Chalmers, surprised at the venom coming from him. It threw him off to have the courtly elderly man treat him like gum on the sidewalk.

"Okay then… uh… my plan is to approach the Big Man, and get him to officially release these two operatives from duty, so that they can live as normal a life as possible, and…"

Chalmers held up a hand, stopping him.

"That's already been taken care of. He was here the day that you were captured, and had granted full independence, including the return of their erased identities, to Spencer and Janssen should they so choose to accept them."

He pulled a file from a drawer and placed two documents in front of the stunned Marine. The documents were inscribed on creamy parchment and adorned with a seal that few people are ever privileged enough to see. Spencer was speechless, a feeling that he couldn't quite decipher curling in the pit of his stomach.

"Well, that's that, then," Steve said, rising to go.

"That is by no means that," Chalmers corrected with a raised eyebrow, looking much like a stern principal who was about to assign community service. "Sit down, Mr. Arnold."

Steve sat.

"There were many things, aside from Spencer and Janssen, which were discussed during his brief but productive visit. One of those things was what should be done with you."

"Me?"

"You. It seems that your usefulness to Command has been compromised, so you'll be coming to work for me, despite some reservations that I have regarding your tactics and conduct. Spencer is my lead operative, so everything that you do will need to be cleared by him."

"But, I…"

"Don't interrupt," Chalmers directed, his gaze steady. "You will begin here as an entry-level operative with limited access to sensitive information. This is because I simply don't trust you. You won't be assigned to a permanent position until I am satisfied that your motives and conduct will be above reproach."

"What if I refuse?" some of Steve's former bluster reared its ugly head.

"You will be exiled in order to protect national security. Your American citizenship will be revoked and you will be taken into custody if you even attempt to return to this country."

"You can't do that," Steve narrowed his eyes in challenge.

"Correct, I can't, but those who can have already put the plan in motion. You have two choices… sign on with Beckett Holdings, or leave your country, effective immediately."

"You can't enforce that," was the weak reply.

"Correct again," Chalmers nodded, cutting his eyes in Spencer's direction.

"Seriously? You'd send him after me? This is so messed up," the beaten man shook his head.

"Your new identity is in this envelope, should you decide to leave," the former manservant pushed a manila envelope across the desk.

"I'll stay," Steve muttered, opening up a whole new realm of responsibility for Spencer.

"Wise choice. Step outside the study. There will be an armed operative waiting to escort you to your training. Should you try to elude him, you will be caught and exiled. This is the end of the line, Mr. Arnold. The sooner you accept that, the better your life will be," Chalmers then looked pointedly at the door.

Steve, in a move that no one had anticipated, stood up and stuck his hand out to Spencer, who shook it. "Good luck on the outside, Marine. You more than earned it," he said quietly, then turned and left the room.

Chalmers' phone vibrated and he glanced at it quickly, the color draining from his face.

"What is it?" Spencer demanded.

"It's Janssen. He's septic. They have him on the strongest antibiotics in modern medicine, but he's not breathing on his own. It doesn't look good son, I'm sorry," Chalmers took off his glasses and cleared his throat. "Our government has granted us permission to go after the two foreign operatives who kidnapped him and Steve Arnold, if you're so inclined."

"I'm not going anywhere until Janssen recovers," Spencer promised, teeth clenched, eye muscle twitching.

"There's a very good chance that…" Chalmers began.

"No!" Spencer shot to his feet and headed for the door. "He's not going down. Not like that," he growled and left the room, the heavy mahogany door swinging shut behind him.

CHAPTER 13

"**P**etaluma, how lovely to see you," Missy lied, astonished that Grayson's mother was up before noon and was standing in her cupcake shop.

"Coffee smells good, and after that husband of yours kept me locked up like a bad dog all night, you might want to throw in some breakfast too," the unkempt woman eyed the display cases.

"Of course, won't you sit down with us?" she invited, shooting Echo a warning look.

"Might as well," was the muttered response as Petaluma flopped into a chair across from Echo. "What are you lookin' at?" she challenged.

"You really don't want me to answer that," Echo raised an eyebrow, having no patience for her belligerence.

"Here we go," Missy trilled, placing a plate with two cupcakes, and a cup of coffee in front of Grayson's mother, who promptly swiped her forefinger into the frosting and sucked it into her mouth.

"Not bad," she commented, taking another glob and rinsing it down with coffee.

"I'm glad you like it," Missy forced a smile as she watched a glob of fluffy white frosting slide slowly down the side of the coffee mug.

"So when are we gonna finish gettin' things set up for the weddin?" Petaluma asked, taking a monster bite out of her nearly naked cupcake.

"Oh, you don't have to worry about that. All of the arrangements are finalized."

"We'll see about that," she made a face. "I ain't got a dress yet."

"Oh, well… uh…" Missy faltered, not knowing what to say. She certainly didn't want to go shopping, but she felt like she had at least some degree of responsibility toward the woman.

"So, how'd you get out of jail?" Echo broke in, savoring a bite of her cupcake and saving her friend from having to form an awkward answer.

"Cuz I ain't guilty, that's why," Petaluma bristled, crumbs of cupcake falling from her mouth into her coffee mug.

"Then why did they take you in?" the hormonal redhead persisted, seemingly trying to provoke Grayson's mother. Missy nudged her under the table with her foot and gave her another warning look.

"Maybe somebody who was out to get me called in a filthy, lyin' anonymous report," her smoker's voice dripped with sarcasm. "Y'all know anybody who'd do such a thing?" she stared at Echo.

The door bells jangled, sparing a response, and the three women looked up to see Sarah walk in, her face turning white when she spotted Petaluma.

"Oh! Mrs. Myers... hi," she stammered, looking desperately at Missy and Echo for support.

Echo looked ready to pounce if need be, and Petaluma responded in a way that shocked them all.

"Sarah, my baby girl..." she leapt up from her chair to lock the surprised bride-to-be in a less than fragrant embrace, bursting into tears.

Sarah peered over her future mother-in-law's shoulder, eyes wide, patting the woman's back awkwardly and meeting Echo and Missy's stunned gazes.

"It's so good to see you. Is my boy with you? Is my Gray here? Where is he? He needs to come give his mama some sugar," Petaluma held Sarah's face between her smoke-stained hands, breathing foul breath into the poor girl's face.

"Uh, no, he's not here yet," Sarah replied, as polite as always, but clearly uncomfortable. "Umm... how are you?"

"I'd be better if everyone in the town stopped tryin' to blame stuff on me that I didn't do," her expression turned sour, and Sarah shifted her feet uncertainly, not knowing what to say.

"Sarah, honey, would you like a cupcake?" Missy asked, rescuing her.

"Oh, no thank you, I have to get going, actually. I'm… uh…" she looked over at Echo who subtly shook her head in warning. "I'm meeting a friend," she finished, not revealing that she was meeting Izzy to go dress shopping.

"All right, dearie," Petaluma grabbed her again, hugging her close. "You go have fun while you're still young and free. We can go over the weddin' stuff when you get back."

Sarah scooted out rather quickly, and Petaluma stuffed her remaining cupcake in her mouth, leaving soon after, mumbling something about time with her man.

"Why do you suppose Chas let her go?" Echo wondered when Grayson's mother left, leaving a trail of cupcake crumbs in her wake.

"I guess she wasn't guilty," Missy shrugged. "I'm glad about that, for Grayson's sake, but it really makes me wonder who would do something so awful to such a sweet girl."

"Maybe it was the boyfriend after all," Echo mused.

"Maybe."

***

Timothy Eckels was surprised when he saw the results of the testing that he'd ordered as a typical part of his autopsy. He flagged the hair samples found on the body, as well as the scrapings under Nari Lee's fingernails, thinking that those particular results would be of interest to Detective Beckett, and finished preparing his report. He'd send it over via email immediately, and have Fiona deliver a hard copy to the police station.

***

Chas Beckett sat across from Logan Greitzer and Marty Nussbaum once again, this time ready for some answers.

"Did you bring the tape?" he asked, wasting no time with pleasantries.

"I did, and we'll be happy to share it with you as soon as you produce a signature on the agreement that I sent you two days ago," Nussbaum's face was like stone and Logan merely looked bored.

"Here it is," Chas slapped the paper down casually on the desk. "But you might want to advise your client that, while we have agreed not to bring charges based upon anything we see in the tape, we reserve the right to prosecute for any future actions which are the same or similar. You'll read that in the addendum from the DA," the detective warned.

"Yes, I'm aware of the provision," Marty replied dryly, scanning the agreement. "Shall we proceed?" he asked unlocking his briefcase.

"By all means," Chas sighed. "Let's get this over with."

The detective sat, his face registering no reaction, as he observed, courtesy of a hidden videocamera, more than one illegal activity that took place in Logan Greitzer's bedroom on the night of Nari Lee's murder. Chas was certain that Logan's paid companion was unaware of the camera's existence. There were hours of footage which covered the entire window of opportunity for the murder. Rather than watching it all in real time, the detective fast-forwarded through the debauchery, resigned to the fact that it provided proof that Logan could not possibly be Nari's killer.

Chas switched off the screen and tented his fingers under his chin, gazing at Logan speculatively.

"So, we're done here?" Marty asked as a formality, already gathering his things.

"Why were you trying to break into the Lee residence?" the detective ignored the attorney, directing his attention to Logan.

"I was looking for something," the young man sighed.

"What were you looking for?"

"You don't have to answer that," Marty chimed in, an automatic response.

"A necklace," Logan shrugged.

"Why?"

"You don't have to answer that," Marty parroted. Logan rolled his eyes.

"Because I had given it to her and it was expensive. Since she wasn't going to need it anymore, I figured I could pawn it or something."

"Describe it," Chas leaned forward.

"It was her initial, a letter N with diamonds."

Chas nodded. "Okay. I'll be in touch if I need anything else."

Marty stopped at the door. "Remember, nothing that you saw on that tape…"

"What tape?" Chas said tiredly, knowing how the game was played.

"Exactly," the lawyer grinned like a Cheshire cat.

Chas watched them go, tapping his pen on his blotter. It would have been so much easier if Logan had been the perpetrator. All the evidence now pointed to Petaluma, perhaps with Steve acting as her sidekick, but something about the whole thing just seemed rather… off. While Grayson's mother had a temper and a profound lack of judgment, she didn't seem like the type who had so much latent rage built up inside that she'd go out of her way to murder a young woman with whom she'd clashed over flowers.

Chuck Sardo, one of the lab techs, poked his head into the detective's office and rapped lightly on the door frame.

"Detective Beckett… if you have a minute, I have the lab results back in the Lee case," he announced. "We're still waiting for the stuff from the coroner, but I can give you what we've got so far."

"Sure, Chuck. Have a seat," Chas stretched, rolling his neck from side to side, hoping that the lab results would make the case easier to solve rather than more difficult. "What do we have?"

The tech handed over a copy of the report so that the detective could follow along as he walked him through it.

"Well, I found fingerprints on the pocket knife, as well as a bit of DNA."

"And?"

"And they belong to a Steven Stoughton."

"Loud Steve," Chas sighed, shaking his head.

"I'm sorry?" Chuck was confused.

"Nothing. Go on."

"There were hairs in the victim's bedroom that were a DNA match for Petaluma Myers, and the weapon recovered at Steven Stoughton's residence had traces of the victim's blood on it."

The detective nodded, thinking.

"What about the necklace?"

"The necklace had a partial print on it that we haven't been able to match to anything in the database," Chuck replied.

"And the two samples of hair that I gave you yesterday?"

"One was a match for Petaluma Myers, the other wasn't in our database."

Chas frowned and closed the manila folder, lost in though.

"Thanks. Let me know when the coroner's labs come in," the detective said absently, staring into space.

CHAPTER 14

C has Beckett was really not looking forward to this particular interview, but he had to ensure justice was served in the Nari Lee case, so he stuck one finger out and rang Loud Steve's doorbell. Petaluma answered the door and made an angry sound the moment that she saw him.

"Oh no, not you again! I'm so sick of seeing cops at my door, this is harassment. I don't care if Grayson thinks you're the next best thing to sliced bread, I will press charges and sue you for every dime you've got. I'm a citizen, you can't treat me like this," she railed, and Chas was pleased to see that, while irate, she seemed sober.

"Ms. Myers, I'm simply here to talk to you. There are several pieces of evidence linking you to Nari Lee's murder, and if you didn't do it, we need to sit down and figure out how and why that happened," the detective explained calmly, wedging his foot in the door frame so that she couldn't close the door.

"You mean you came to your senses and think I'm innocent?" she narrowed her eyes.

"I'm willing to give you another chance to go through your story and see if there's anything that you haven't told me."

"Baby, what's goin' on out there?" Steve rumbled up behind Petaluma, putting his hands protectively on her shoulders.

"This cop that my son is so fond of wants to talk to me again."

"Actually, I'd like to talk to both of you if you don't mind?"

"Bout what?" Steve's tone was borderline belligerent.

"About whether you'd like to cooperate with me in finding out the truth or whether you'd like to go back to jail right now," Chas raised an eyebrow.

Steve let out an exaggerated sigh.

"Let him in, let's get this over with. Those bunks at the jail make my lower back hurt," he muttered, heading toward the living room.

The three of them sat in a crumb-strewn, humid living room.

"Do you have a pearl-handled pocket knife?" Chas asked Steve point-blank.

"Yup, sure do. Little bitty thing. Had it since I was a kid. Keep it on my nightstand, cuz you never know when it might come in handy for openin' a bag of chips or something. Why?"

"Can you go get it for me?" the detective asked.

"All right, but it ain't big enough to give you much more than a paper cut," Steve muttered, lumbering toward the bedroom.

"Have you had any other strange or suspicious encounters since the day of the murder?" Chas asked Petaluma while Steve was out of the room.

"Nope, life's been pretty quiet around here. We've just been spending some quality time together if you know what I mean," she gave Chas a lopsided grin.

"I can't find the dang thing," Steve came back into the room, a bit out of breath. "I looked on the night stand, in it, and on the floor. Did you borrow it, sugarcakes?"

"Nope, haven't seen it. Hey, has anything weird happened around her since that girl got killed?"

"Depends on your definition of weird," he waggled his eyebrows suggestively at Petaluma, who giggled. "There was that one hostile delivery guy that came by though, did he ever give you the food?"

"Hostile delivery guy?" Chas interrupted before she could answer.

"Yeah, this dude had an attitude problem and was talking nonsense. I don't think he even gave us our Chinese food."

"What do you mean by "talking nonsense?" the detective leaned forward.

"He was hollerin' somethin' about us being sorry, but he hadn't even asked for the money yet, and we tried to pay him.

"Can you describe him?"

Steve and Petaluma gave as much of a description as they could, their memories fogged by alcohol.

"Yeah, he was a nasty one," Petaluma nodded. "Grabbed me by the shoulder and darn near tore my hair out. He had some serious anger issues. So now what? You gonna take us to jail again? I hope y'all got better food this time around, that meat loaf was the saddest thing I ever saw."

"No, I may be back to ask you some more questions though, so just sit tight for a bit," Chas advised.

"We ain't goin' nowhere, 'cept maybe to the fridge for more beers," she giggled, casting adoring glances at the belching man beside her.

***

Chas sat at his desk, thinking that he'd just confirmed his worst suspicions, but not wanting to believe it.

Chuck Sardo appeared in his doorway again. "Hey, Detective. I've got the report back from the coroner, and we've found some interesting coincidences in the evidence."

"I don't believe in coincidences," Chas remarked, taking the report. "What do we have?"

"A few notable things. The hair samples that you provided match both the ones that the coroner found and the ones that were found in the victim's bedroom. All of this may or may not be interesting, depending upon where your hair samples came from. Some belong to Petaluma Myers, others match each other, but aren't known in the database. We also traced a footprint that was near the bush where the murder weapon was found, to a highly expensive Italian shoe, size nine. Might want to check the size of Logan Greitzer's feet," Sardo suggested.

Chas nodded, staring down at the report without seeing it, his mind buzzing and whirring as he put the pieces of the puzzle together. "Did we get the video surveillance tapes from the bar where the bloody linens were found in the dumpster?"

"Yeah, strange thing about that. The uniforms who went over there spoke with every person on staff and everyone denied making the call. The one male bartender and manager that they have were working that night, and footage from inside the bar shows that they couldn't have made the call. The rest of the staff is female, which makes me wonder who called in the anonymous tip and said that they were a bartender? Looks like Logan again."

"I think I have a pretty good idea," the detective sighed.

"There's one other thing that could be pretty important."

"Yeah, what's that?"

"The victim was pregnant. The DNA test that the coroner did on the fetus matched the unknown hair sample DNA, and the unknown blood sample at the scene."

Chas let out a breath. "Okay. Thanks, Chuck," he said, dismissing the tech.

The detective reviewed the tape from the bar, reviewed additional surveillance from the flower shop, and knew what he had to do.

***

"Mr. and Mrs. Lee… there's been a break in the case that I'd like to share with you, may I come in?" Detective Chas Beckett stood on the doorstep of the Lee residence.

"Of course, please come in," Mrs. Lee gestured for him to follow her, looking anxious. "Can I get you some tea?" she asked, while the detective seated himself in the living room with her husband.

"No, I'm fine, thanks, but I'm wondering if you might be able to answer a few questions for me."

"Of course, anything we can do to help," Mr. Lee agreed quickly. "You said you had a break in the case?"

"Yes, we'll get to that," Chas assured him as Mrs. Lee sat on the couch with her husband. "Mrs. Lee, did you realize that your daughter was pregnant at the time of her death?"

The color drained from her face. "It was that horrible boy wasn't it? It was that awful Logan Greitzer, he killed my daughter and my grandchild," she whispered, her hands going to her throat in horror.

"I'm sorry, I know this must be a horrible shock for you," the detective said quietly before continuing. "Mrs. Lee, how would you characterize your marriage?" he asked, clearly surprising them.

"My marriage?" she was clearly puzzled and reached for Jeong's hand. "We have a good marriage… what does that have to do with anything?"

"I'm sorry, Detective, but that question is out of line for a grieving family. What are you thinking?" Mr. Lee frowned, clutching his wife's hand.

"I'm thinking that your relationship with your stepdaughter may have been a bit strained, Mr. Lee. Would you say that's a fair assessment?" Chas stared him down.

"Nari was a pretty typical young adult, she resisted authority and rules on occasion, but I wouldn't say our relationship was strained," Jeong shook his head. "Why would you say such a thing at a time like this?"

"Did you ever argue?"

"Don't all parents and kids?"

"Did the conflict ever become physical?"

"Don't be ridiculous," he sputtered. "You need to tell us what the break in the case is and then leave. I won't have you insulting my family while we grieve.

"You want to know about the break in the case? I'll tell you about the break in the case. I've discovered, through a substantial amount of evidence, who your daughter's killer is," he addressed Mrs. Lee.

"Mr. Lee, you disappeared for about an hour while we were investigating your home, right before you and Mrs. Lee left town. Can you tell me where you were?"

"Of course. I was trying to be helpful, I went to get a copy of the videotape from the floral shop surveillance, in case there were any clues on it. I turned it over to you immediately."

"Did you? Or did you watch it while you were still in the shop?"

Jeong blinked for a moment. "Well, obviously I reviewed the footage at the shop. How could I have known that there was a suspicious interaction if I didn't see the tape?"

"And then you went to the visitor's log and saw the names of the three ladies who had been in the shop for a consultation that day."

"Yes, I thought you might need to speak with them."

"Then you tracked down Petaluma Myers and confronted her."

"I did no such thing," Jeong protested, growing visibly agitated.

"Sure you did. You confronted Petaluma, and when you met her you figured she'd be an easy suspect to setup. You made certain that when she walked away from you, you pulled out some strands of her hair, so that you could come back here and plant them in your stepdaughter's room. Sometime after that, you went back to the house where Petaluma was staying, and I'm guessing that you broke in when no one was home."

"This is ridiculous, I won't stand for..." Jeong rose to his feet, red-faced.

"You're right, Jeong, you won't stand. You're going to sit down and let me finish," Chas stood and towered over him until he sat. His wife didn't take his hand this time.

"When you broke into the house, you planted Nari's necklace behind the dresser—it had your fingerprint on it—and you took a pocketknife that you later claimed you had found in your stepdaughter's bedroom, and turned it in as evidence."

"My husband would never do such a thing, Detective. He loved Nari, he would never..."

"That's not all he did, Mrs. Lee. The murder weapon, which was taken from your kitchen and had your daughter's DNA on it, was found buried under a bush behind the house that he broke into. You know what else was under that bush, Mrs. Lee? A shoeprint. A size nine shoeprint from an Italian shoe that looks just like that," Chas pointed to Jeong's cordovan loafers.

"That's ridiculous. I didn't kill Nari, it had to be that boy she was dating. He always seemed violent," Mr. Lee found his voice again.

"Yes, you thought that you were one step ahead of us by implicating Logan Greitzer as the killer, but you weren't quite as careful as you thought you were. You called in an anonymous tip and claimed to be a bartender at the bar where the linens from Nari's bed were found in the dumpster. We knew we'd been set up when we interviewed the only two male employees of that bar and watched video of their movements on the night in question, which proved that neither one of them could have made the call. What you didn't know, was that they had cameras recording the rear of the bar by the dumpsters as well. When we saw the figure on the video, wouldn't you know, it looked an awful lot like the figure who had been on video at the floral shop. So you tried to set up Logan and you tried to set up Petaluma to point us in the wrong direction, and you succeeded for a while," Chas regarded the stepfather darkly.

"But, he loved Nari... how do you know it was him. It could've been anyone? He loved her," Mrs. Lee protested, tears running down her cheeks.

"Mrs. Lee, I'm sorry, but we found hair samples of your husband's at the crime scene, in the bathroom where the body was found, and at the residence where Petaluma Myers is staying. We know it was him, because when he came to see me at the station, I took his jacket to hang it up. On the jacket were his hairs and hairs from Petaluma Myers. Apparently he'd worn the jacket when he went to see her, or when he planted her hairs in your daughter's room. I sent the hairs to the lab for analysis, and the results confirmed my suspicions," the detective replied grimly.

"How could you do this? Why would you do this?" she clutched at her husband's arm, sobbing. "You didn't really do it, Jeong, did you?" she pleaded. "Detective, this doesn't make sense, what reason could my Jeong possibly have to do such a thing?"

"The fetus that your daughter carried shared your husband's DNA, Mrs. Lee. I'm very sorry."

"No, no... no..." she rose from the couch and started shaking her head, backing away from the monster sitting next to her. "Nooo!" she screamed and ran toward the bedroom.

"Cecilia... wait," Jeong stood, moving as though he planned to go after her and Chas grabbed him, lightning fast, pinning his arms behind him.

"Jeong Lee, you are under arrest for the murder of Nari Lee," he began, and read the prisoner his rights.

CHAPTER 15

The dark shadow of three days of growth graced the chiseled planes of Spencer Bengal's weary face, as he gazed down at Janssen's pale form. The scarred and injured Marine had been taken off of the ventilator, and was breathing on his own, but had remained in a medically induced coma until today. The staff doctor at the Beckett estate had stopped the drugs that were keeping Janssen asleep, and Spencer was waiting to see if his buddy would wake up or not. The doc had said that if it didn't happen in the next twenty-four hours, chances were slim that it would ever happen. So Spencer waited, not leaving the room for any reason, standing vigil for his fallen friend.

His head ached, his back ached, and his stomach growled, but even Chalmers hadn't been able to convince him to leave Janssen's side. He had to know that the Marine was going to be all right, and he irrationally felt that his presence might help somehow. Couldn't hurt anyway. So many thoughts had gone through his mind while he waited faithfully for his friend to awaken. He'd thought of Izzy and the wonderful times that they'd had, he thought of dark things from his past, and of the positive things from the present—Missy, Chas, Echo… having a family again. He didn't know much about Janssen, other than that he hadn't been able to assimilate back into real life after Afghanistan, but he knew that the battle-hardened young man had saved his life, and the lives of others more than once.

Spencer paced about the room, lost in thought and frustrated that Janssen wasn't waking up. It had been hours since the meds were stopped, and still… nothing.

"Gimme a beer," a weak voice rasped from behind him, startling him from his reverie.

He whirled around to see Janssen blinking to clear his vision, half of his mouth raised in a crooked smile.

"Bout time you decided to join the living again," Spencer ambled to his bedside, as if he wasn't concerned at all. An emotional reaction was not what his buddy needed at the moment, so he contented himself with a handshake. "Welcome back, man. We missed you."

"Had to take some drastic measures to get a good nap," Janssen replied.

"I can't get you that beer just yet, but how about some water?"

"Definitely. And sit this thing up, I can't see anything when I'm flat on my back."

Spencer pressed the foot pedal on the bed, raising the top half.

"I'll be right back," he promised, leaving the room for the first time in a long time, in search of water.

Janssen was monitored via video, twenty-four hours a day, and as soon as Spencer left the room, the doctor hurried toward it, eager to check on his patient. When he returned, the doc was giving his buddy an exam.

"How are you feeling?" the doctor asked, flashing a light into Janssen's eyes.

"Thirsty. When are you gonna pull these wires outta me so that I can get going?" he grumbled as the doctor listened to his breathing.

"We'll do some labs to make certain that the infection is entirely cleared up, we'll get you gradually back on solid foods, and then we'll give you one last physical to assess your condition overall. Should only be a few days," he assured him.

"A few days? I'm ready for solid food now. Spence, order me a pizza, man."

"Not happening. You were in bad shape, gotta listen to the doc on this one," Spencer grinned.

"You just wait 'til I get out of this bed," he groused, then took the straw that Spencer offered, drinking refreshingly cool water.

"Not too much at first," the doctor warned. "We have to proceed slowly, your body's been through a lot."

"Compared to being trapped in a cage in the desert, I'd say this wasn't so bad," Janssen muttered.

"You were younger then," the doctor tossed over his shoulder as he left the room. "Remember, you're being monitored."

"Big Brother is watching," Spencer added, chuckling and holding Janssen's cup near him so that he could continue to sip.

"Indeed," the doctor closed the door on his way out.

Janssen drank deeply, and Spencer put the cup on a table across the room.

"Benedict Arnold," the scarred Marine grumbled.

"Just following orders," Spencer replied.

"Since when have you ever followed orders?"

"Since my invincible buddy almost got taken out by infected wounds," he sobered. "You had a close call, man. I was worried."

"Well, there's no reason to go all mother hen on me," Janssen smiled faintly, clearly feeling better after the water. "Shoulda known I'd make it, I always do."

"I think you've used up about seven or eight of your nine lives right about now," Spencer gave him a pointed look.

"Doesn't mean I'm gonna stop doing what I do," he shrugged, wincing a bit at the pain in his arm.

"At least now you'll have a choice."

"What's that supposed to mean?" Janssen's eyes narrowed.

"We've got documents from Command. They cut us loose, permanently. They can ask us to volunteer for missions, but if we refuse, they leave us alone. We're free, buddy. We're finally free," Spencer's voice trailed off to a whisper, and Janssen stared at him in disbelief.

"You got it in writing?"

"Yep, the Big Man came down here personally," he nodded.

"So when I leave here…"

"You can go wherever you want to go. No more running, no more hiding. You can even have your own name back if you want it. They'll reinstate our identities. I'll wait until you're able to travel before I head out of here. You have any idea what you want to do?"

Janssen nodded, his throat working. The toughened and scarred Marine's eyes inexplicably filled with tears. "I'm going home," he husked. "I'm finally going home."

***

Spencer walked into the bus station more slowly than he normally would, because Janssen still had a significant limp. It would be gone eventually, but the Marine still had some healing to do. Janssen bought his ticket, and Spencer teased him for it.

"You know, with what you got from the good old USA and Beckett Holdings, you could afford to charter a plane to get back home."

Janssen shifted his backpack over his good shoulder and nodded.

"Yeah, I know, but this'll give me time to get used to being around people again, and to work up the guts to go home."

"Have you called her?" Spencer's eyes were grave.

Janssen shook his head, his eyes pained.

"Nah. If I do this, I'm just gonna show up. See if she still wants to see me," he said softly, looking vulnerable for probably the first time in his life.

"Of course she'll want to see you. What are you talking about?" Spencer chastised him lightly.

"I'm not like I was. I let her think I died over there, so she wouldn't get hurt by the guys who were trying to hunt me down. I lied to her by not coming back to her, and then I show up out of the blue, looking like this," he swallowed hard, looking away.

Spencer tilted his head back to the ceiling and took a deep breath, trying to get his emotions under control, then decided, for both of their sakes, to lighten up a bit.

"Well, it's not like you were that great looking to start with, man," he teased, swallowing the lump in his throat.

Before Janssen could answer, the loudspeaker blared that it was time to board. The two men stood looking at each other for a long moment, then Spencer stepped forward and wrapped his brother-at-arms in a bear hug.

"I'm gonna miss you, not even lying," he ground out, unashamed of the tears in his cobalt eyes.

"Right back atcha, brother. I'll always have your back, count on that," Janssen replied hoarsely, hugging him back fiercely, despite the pain in his arm.

They clapped each other on the back a couple of times and broke apart, wiping their eyes, because that's what men do.

"Take care, Janssen," Spencer's jaw flexed as his heart broke, wondering if he'd ever see him again.

Unable to form a reply, Janssen bumped his fist over his heart twice and turned away, the doors of the bus closing behind him.

Spencer didn't stay to see his face in the window one last time… he couldn't. He barely made it to his car before breaking down and letting out the sobs that he'd been keeping inside for far too many years. This was the end of an era, and the beginning of his new life.

CHAPTER 16

Echo saw Spencer slip into the back of the Wedgewood Parlor at the Inn, where Grayson and Sarah's wedding ceremony had just begun, and beckoned him to come sit by her. Kel was on her left, and Joyce, her store manager, was on her right. When Spencer ducked into the row, Joyce scooted over so that he could sit between her and Echo.

The bride was radiantly beautiful, and Grayson looked handsome, if slightly uncomfortable in his dove grey tux. The ceremony was heartfelt, and there wasn't a dry eye in the room after the bride and groom said their handwritten vows to each other. Petaluma sat in the front, and she had actually managed to get Loud Steve into a tie. Missy and Chas sat across the aisle from them in the front as well.

A few rows back sat a clearly introverted Timothy Eckels, escorted by his lovely assistant, Fiona, who had worn pink, as Sarah had requested in the invitation. Almost every woman in the room wore pink, and the appearance was that of a festive bouquet. Petaluma's dress was neon pink and covered in sequins, ending way above the knee, which Steve caressed throughout the ceremony. Missy and Chas had flown Grayson's entire staff up from Louisiana as a surprise, and there were several police officers in attendance as well, because Missy loved any chance to throw a great party and figured the more the merrier.

After Spencer had gratefully accepted hugs from Echo and Joyce and shaken Kel's hand, all without disturbing the ceremony, he faced the front and immediately saw the back of a head that he would know anywhere. Izzy. She looked beautiful in pink, and almost as if she felt his presence from across the room, she glanced back and saw Spencer, her mouth falling open in surprise for a moment. She raised her hand in greeting and he returned the small wave, not knowing what to think when she turned back around. His heart beat fast in his chest. He'd forgotten that Izzy might be at the wedding, and hadn't prepared himself emotionally for seeing her again so soon.

After the ceremony, the bride and groom were whisked away to take pictures on the lovely grounds and on the beach. Missy caught sight of Spencer and made a beeline for him, dragging Chas behind her.

"Oh my darlin' boy, I've been so worried about you," she cried, throwing her arms around the Marine. "I can't believe you're back. Are you staying? Are you okay? Do you need anything?" she peppered him with questions, her head on his chest.

"Sweetie, let him breathe for a second," Chas chuckled, and Missy stood back with a laugh.

"I'm sorry, sugar, I'm just so glad to see you," she wiped her eyes. "Land sakes, at the end of this day I'm not going to have any mascara left at all."

Chas looked at Spencer and wordlessly enveloped him in a hug.

"You good?" he asked in a low voice.

"Yes sir, for the first time in a long time, I'm good," the Marine replied.

"Good, then let's head to the bar and get you a drink," the detective grinned, spiriting the young man away.

"That's the best idea I've heard all day," Spencer agreed, falling in step.

"Good lord, who is that fine young thang?" Petaluma drawled when he passed by her, drawing a kicked-puppy look from Steve.

"It's just me," Chas joked, still walking.

"Twenty years ago, maybe," was the saucy reply.

The two men ordered their drinks and stood off to the side of the bar, tasting their first sips.

"You back for good?" Chas asked lightly.

"If you'll have me. Did you hear from Chalmers?"

The detective nodded. "I'm kind of surprised that you're staying with us when you could literally go anywhere in the world and do anything you like. I'm grateful, just surprised."

"I have a purpose here. I'm needed. And you guys are family. Why would I walk away from that?"

"I'm glad you feel that way, Spence. Our door is always open to you," Chas raised his glass, and Spencer clinked it with his own.

"Thank you sir."

"Stop calling me sir."

"Yes sir," he grinned.

Izzy had just gotten a drink from the bar and approached the two men like a shy doe.

"Hi. I don't want to interrupt," she said softly, staring at Spencer.

"Not at all," Chas replied smoothly. "I was just leaving to go find my wife, but I'm sure this young man will talk your ear off."

He shook Spencer's hand, smiled at Izzy and went on his way.

"Hi," she said again.

"Hi."

"Can we talk for a minute?" she asked, visibly trying not to fidget.

"Sure," the Marine nodded, taking another swig of his Manhattan.

"Do you... that is, can we... ?" she gestured vaguely to the French doors which led to the patio.

"Uh, yeah, I could use some fresh air," Spencer replied, gallantly giving her his arm.

She looked beautiful, but he was certain that she was unaware of it. Whenever he saw raw beauty in her, she noticed stray hairs, a wrinkle in her blouse, and flat feet.

"Do you want to sit?" he asked, gesturing to a bistro table which had been set up for wedding guests who wanted to spend some time outdoors.

"Umm... no, let's go stand under the trees, in the shade," Izzy suggested, pointing to an area far away from any other wedding guests.

"Lead the way."

They stood under the tree just looking at each other for a moment before Izzy spoke.

"I'm sorry," she said, her eyes moist.

"About?"

"About... the way I treated you, the way I acted... how I sent you away. I was awful to you, and I'm sorry about that," she bit her lip in that way that he'd once found so endearing.

"It's okay. I can't imagine what it must've been like for you. I'm sorry that you got wrapped up in that whole mess. It was my fault, I should have known better than to get involved with anyone."

"Well... that's what I wanted to talk with you about, actually," Izzy took his hand.

"What?"

"I had made up my mind that I was not going to deal with all of the drama that you brought in to my life, that I wouldn't put up with a man who made me concerned for my own safety all the time, even if it wasn't exactly his fault... I had written you... written us... off. But then, when I came home and you weren't here, I missed you so much, and I realized that... I really do love you, and I'm willing to be there for you, even in spite of the bad guys who break into my house and kidnap me," she grinned wryly. "Spence, I want to try again. We can do this."

Spencer gazed into those beautiful hazel eyes, then squeezed her hand gently and let it drop.

"Izzy... you wanted to know about my past... and I never told you everything. I told you mostly everything, but not everything. One of the things that you didn't know, is that I was very much in love once, a long time ago. She was an amazing woman who loved me with all of her heart. She stood by me through thick and thin, and put up with things that no one else ever had, or ever would. She held me when I woke up screaming in the night, and welcomed me home when I'd just disappear without a trace for a few days. She showed me unconditional love, and I walked away from it, because I wanted to protect her. I was wrong to do that. She didn't want me to protect her, she just wanted to be with me, but I couldn't handle it, for whatever reason, and I walked away."

"Oh Spencer, I'm sorry," she whispered, touching his suit jacket. "What happened to her?"

"She married my buddy, they had a kid," he gave a humorless laugh.

"Oh gosh, I'm so sorry, but I'm so glad that you shared that with me. I think it's a good start. You can just tell me about things from your past whenever you're ready. One thing at a time," she squeezed his arm through the jacket.

He put his hand briefly over hers, then let it drop.

"Izzy, I told you that to let you know that I've experienced unconditional love. I know what it's like, I've lived it. I poured my heart out to you more than once, and you left me without a backward glance. I'm not saying that to accuse you, it's just reality. When you left me at the airport that last time, a little part of me died, a part that I really couldn't afford to lose. So, I put whatever I had felt for you into a little box deep inside and left it there until the feelings went away," Spencer explained gently. "You're a sweet person, with so much to offer to someone, but I'm sorry Izzy, that someone isn't me. If you ever need anything, I'll try my best to be there for you, but I'm sorry, there's no going back this time."

He leaned over and kissed her forehead gently. As she stared into his eyes, he brushed her cheek with the back of his hand, then turned away, heading back toward the reception. She ducked between the bushes and ran from the Inn, dodging trees and shrubs in her haste to get away before the tears started. Spencer reached the doors to go inside, feeling as though a great weight had been lifted. Endings hurt, but they also led to new beginnings.

Joyce Rutledge was standing just inside the French doors when Spencer came back in. She looked him up and down twice, nodding her satisfaction.

"You look like a man who needs a good meal," she observed, hands on hips.

"I could eat," Spencer nodded, glad for the distraction of her delightful company. Her bubblegum pink chiffon gown looked amazing against her mocha skin, and her smile lit the room.

"Then come with me, handsome," she commanded, grabbing his hand and leading him away.

"Where are we going?" he grinned, allowing himself to be towed along behind her.

"There's a buffet over there that's begging to be raided. We're going to show 'em how it's done, sunshine."

***

Echo and Kel were on the dance floor, swaying together and gazing lovingly into each other's eyes, when suddenly all the color drained from Echo's face and she looked terrified.

Kel stopped dancing immediately.

"What is it, love?" he asked, frowning with concern.

"Something's wrong," she said, clutching her midsection. "I think I might be bleeding," she whispered.

With almost a sixth sense, Missy darted over from across the room, and saw that her best friend was in distress.

"You come with me, darlin," she put her arm around Echo's shoulders, walking slowly toward a fainting couch. "Kel, go get the car and send Spencer over here to carry her to it."

She needn't have requested the second part. Almost as soon as the words were out of her mouth, Spencer and Joyce appeared at her side, their plates left half-empty on the table.

"What do you need?" he asked grimly.

"Kel's bringing the car around, pick her up easy and take her out. I'll be right behind you," Missy instructed. "Joyce, go tell Grayson and Sarah what's going on, but tell them not to worry and that they'd better not miss their flight tomorrow. I'll take care of Echo," she gave hurried instructions.

"I know you will, I've got this," Joyce assured her. "You go. And give her a hug for me. I'll be at the hospital shortly."

Chas stayed, playing the role of an excellent host, until the last guest had gone. Grayson and Sarah were headed to the airport early in the morning, Petaluma and Steve had finally been coaxed into taking a cab home, and the detective headed for the hospital as soon as the door shut behind them. The caterer could clean up the Inn, with Maggie the Innkeeper providing oversight, so Chas joined Missy, Spencer, and Joyce in the waiting room outside the maternity ward.

"What do we know?" he asked, handing each of them a cup of coffee from the cardboard tray that the hospital cafeteria had given him.

"Nothing yet. Kel said that he'd come out and tell us what was going on once the doctor had seen her," Missy's eyes were red, and Chas sat down and put his arm around her.

Spencer and Joyce sat side by side, him staring at the floor, her flipping through the pages of a magazine without seeing them.

"What are we gonna do, Chas? Missy whispered against her husband's chest, tissues clenched in her hand.

"We're going to wait," he said softly, kissing the top of her head.

Joyce sighed shakily and Spencer reached for her hand.

Summer Prescott 2016